BATTLE FOR THE

SOULSPRING

D1407496

STORIES IN AN AGE OF FANTASY

REALM QUEST

STORIES FROM THE FAR FUTURE

WARPED GALAXIES

REALM QUEST

BATTLE FOR THE
SOULSPRING

TOM HUDDLESTON

WARHAMMER ADVENTURES

First published in Great Britain in 2021 by
Warhammer Publishing,
Willow Road,
Nottingham, NG7 2WS, UK.

Represented by: Games Workshop Limited – Irish branch,
Unit 3, Lower Liffey Street, Dublin 1,
D01 K199, Ireland.

10 9 8 7 6 5 4 3 2 1

Produced by Games Workshop in Nottingham.
Cover illustration by Cole Marchetti.
Internal illustrations by Dan Boultwood & Cole Marchetti.

A CIP record for this book is available from the British Library.

ISBN 13: 978 1 78999 069 0

See Warhammer Adventures on the internet at

warhammeradventures.com

Find out more about Games Workshop and the worlds of
Warhammer 40,000 and Warhammer Age of Sigmar at

games-workshop.com

Printed and bound by CPI Group (UK) Ltd, Croydon, CR0 4YY

For Stanley and Frank – my favourite readers.

Contents

The Mortal Realms

Each of the Mortal Realms is a world unto itself, steeped in powerful magic. Seemingly infinite in size, there are endless possibilities for discovery and adventure: floating cities and enchanted woodlands, noble beings and dread beasts beyond imagination. But in every corner of the realms, battles rage between the armies of Order and the forces of Chaos. This centuries-long war must be won if the realms are to live in peace and freedom.

PROLOGUE

Thirty years ago...

The boy felt a cuff on the back of his head and jerked upright.

'Mikal Vertigan, pay attention,' the Oracle snapped. 'This is vitally important.'

He had to admit, his attention had started to wander. It was hard to concentrate on rituals and history when the most beautiful girl in the city of Lifestone – maybe even in the whole realm of Ghyran – was standing so close to him. True, Aisha Sand hadn't so much as glanced his way, but he was sure she wanted to.

'The time has come at last,' the

Oracle continued, turning to face the seven mismatched children standing before her. Moonlight slanted through the windows of the Arbour, gleaming on her black leather brigandine and the silver fountain emblazoned on its breast. 'The time for you to discover your true purpose. To learn why you bear these ancient symbols. To know why the great city of Lifestone has called upon you, this generation's chosen.'

Mikal looked down at his wrist where the mark of Ulgu, Realm of Shadows, shone black against his skin. Beside him, Aisha bore the rune of Shyish, Realm of Death, a fact that seemed to trouble everyone except Vertigan. Some of the other kids were even a little afraid of her, which made no sense to him – sure, she could be a bit snappy sometimes, and she tended to prefer her own company. But he was sure it was just shyness – deep down he knew she was a good person. No one so beautiful could possibly be wicked.

His hand brushed against hers, almost accidentally, and Aisha's grey eyes flashed with annoyance. He gave her what he hoped was a winning smile, and rolled his eyes as if to imply that this was all so boring, and he couldn't wait for it to be over. But the girl looked away, her hands trembling. *That's odd*, he thought. *She seems nervous. Or perhaps she's just excited to see me. Yes, that must be it.*

'To most of you Lifestone is simply the place you were born,' the Oracle was saying. 'But believe me, it is unlike any other city in Ghyran. In towns like Hammerhal or Demesnus the buildings stand straight and tall, arranged in ranks like soldiers. Here in Lifestone they curve and bend, like living trees. In most cities one would use a map to find one's way, and the streets of today would match those of yesterday. In Lifestone things are ever shifting, in ways so subtle that we don't always notice until we set out to find a place and realise it is no longer where it used to be.'

Vertigan had been noticing this peculiar aspect of his home city more and more of late – Lifestone had always been unpredictable, but just recently it had seemed determined to lead him astray, to take him to places he hadn't asked to go. He'd wondered if it was trying to tell him something, but of course that was ridiculous.

'Just two things in Lifestone remain constant,' the Oracle continued. 'The city walls below and this mighty Arbour above, the palace of learning where you have trained these past five years, readying yourself for this great ritual. And now you are ready.'

She pushed open a glass door, beckoning them to follow. Out in the courtyard a spiral grove of slenderwood trees rose from the silver grass, their shadows shifting like spell-runes beneath the waning moon. Somewhere

in the distance Mikal heard the waking
cry of a gyrfalcon, and lifting his gaze
above the dome of the Atheneum he
saw a line of blue and gold tracing
the peaks of the mountains. Dawn was
approaching.

'But what makes our city so different?'
the Oracle asked, stooping to gather
a handful of earth and crumbling
it in her fingers. Mikal smelled the
warm richness of it, mingling with the
familiar scents of bark and sap and
night-blooming cullyflowers.

'It's alive,' he murmured, almost to
himself, and the Oracle smiled.

'Very good,' she said. 'This whole city
is alive. And I don't mean in the sense
that it contains living things, trees
and creatures and mortal folk like us.
Lifestone itself is a living thing, an
entity as old as the realm, its soul
inhabiting every nook and corner of this
blessed place. It gives us sustenance,
it gives us peace, it even gives us
protection, for it is no coincidence that

this is one of the few cities in Ghyran that the forces of Chaos have never conquered.'

She moved across the silent lawn, leading them towards the centre of the courtyard. 'But of course no living thing can give, and give, and require nothing in return. And that is why you are here. Once in every generation seven are called, branded with runes signifying the Mortal Realms – all except Azyr, for no mortal could bear that mark. You come from every walk of life – rich and poor, soldier and healer, educated and unschooled. And when you join together in this sacred place, you allow Lifestone to be reborn.'

A dark shape stood in the open, smooth grey stone against the paling sky. The fountain was carved with the heads of men and beasts – gryph-hounds and drakes, eagles and aurochs. Mikal had always known that this place was somehow the heart of Lifestone – the fountain was on their

banners, their seals, their shields. He'd
even noticed that around the marble
bowl were engraved seven runes, just
like the ones he and his friends bore.
But he'd never known why, until now.

'Find your own mark,' the Oracle told
them. 'Stand before it.'

Vertigan did as she asked, crossing
to the far side of the fountain where
the rune of Ulgu was chiselled into
the marble, a simple downward-facing
spear. It was shimmering, he noticed,
as though mirroring the growing light
in the sky. Across the fountain he saw
Aisha stepping towards the mark of
Shyish, moving hesitantly as though
reluctant to approach the fountain. She
glanced up, meeting his gaze, and for
a moment Mikal's heart stopped. There
was something in Aisha's eyes that he
didn't understand, a look of doubt, even
fear. Then she lowered her head and it
was gone.

'When the first light crests the
mountains, you will be joined,' the

Oracle said, circling behind them. 'And in that joining something magical will be created. A Realmgate, a portal to a place deep inside Ghyran, so deep that mortal eyes will never see it. There lies the Soulspring, a well of life-giving water so pure and untainted that it alone can rejuvenate Lifestone, bringing new life to the everlasting spirit of this great city. Now step forward, and place your hands upon the stone.'

The lip of the fountain was cool beneath Vertigan's palms, and he felt fingers brushing against his own – to his left was Sali, the youngest of them, bearing the mark of Hysh, and to the right stood Kether, a pale boy who carried the rune of Ghur. Mikal felt his mark tingle, as it often did when they were all together. He glanced again at Aisha but her head was still bowed, her mouth moving restlessly as she muttered something under her breath, an inaudible chant. Again he felt a flicker of doubt, but he shook it off as the Oracle raised her hands, sunlight brushing the tips of her fingers.

'Dawn comes,' she said, 'and the gate is opening. I will leave you. This sacred moment is just for the chosen seven. Treasure it, all of you.'

The light touched the peak of the fountain and Mikal felt a sensation pass through him, setting his nerves alight. There was music in the air, a melody like birdsong but deeper somehow, more resonant. Sali laughed and he heard himself doing the same.

The feeling grew more and more intense, as though he were more alive now than he'd ever been, filled from head to toe with growth and spirit and sunlight.

The marble trembled beneath his hands, gently at first then with more force. The rune on his wrist blazed painlessly, seeming to flicker and change. And at the tips of his fingers he saw flashes of azure energy, blue bolts of mystical power rising from within himself and passing to the others on either side. They were connected in a way they'd never been before, but would be forever. It was thrilling beyond measure. He looked from Sali to Gethris to Samkin, seeing the blue light shining in their open eyes, the joy written plain on their sunlit faces.

Then he looked at Aisha, and everything changed.

Her head was still lowered, her fingers gripping the bowl so hard that her knuckles were white. Bolts of power flickered around them but this was darker somehow, a blue so deep it was almost black, coiling round her wrists like rope. The music in the air seemed to speed up, losing its sonorous quality and tipping horribly off-key. Mikal's heartbeat quickened too, racing so fast that it seemed like his chest would burst. The force still rolled through him but now it felt violent somehow, as though he was being buffeted by a fierce gale, a hurricane of mystical energy.

He turned to his friends, trying to work out what was happening, why it all felt so wrong. But they were frozen, their mouths wide as though they wanted to scream but couldn't force the sound out. Aisha raised her head, and terror gripped him.

Her eyes were wide open, staring sightlessly into him. They were black as oil, dark tears rolling down her pale cheeks. The rune on her wrist shone with an ebony light, emitting tendrils of smoke that began to envelop those on either side of her, tightening around them like coils of wire.

Ryla cried out but she could not pull away. The black coils darted from her to Samkin, from Gethris to Sali. Vertigan watched it draw closer, binding the children together, hand to hand. It had Kether now, too – any moment it would reach him. Mikal tried to draw back but he couldn't – some force held him in place, a grim power rooting him to the spot. All he could do was stare at Aisha, pleading with his eyes as her black gaze burrowed through his flesh and right into his soul.

He screamed in horror as the dark force reached for him, flickering around the tips of Sali's fingers. Then somewhere inside him, a quiet voice said, 'No.'

Summoning every bit of strength he had, everything he'd learned from books and training and instinct, Vertigan tore himself away. He reeled back from the fountain, his hands burning with such vivid pain that he thought they might burst into flames. He lost his balance and crashed to the ground, the world tipping and lurching beneath him. For a moment everything spun; he could smell smoke and hear a terrible screaming, a howl of anger and surprise and loss. He knew it was Aisha.

Through the pain and the noise he opened his eyes, trying to stand and failing. The fountain loomed over him, shrouded in darkness. On the far side a pale figure lay in the silver grass, black sparks shooting from her twitching hands. Around her, ringing the fountain, were five slumped forms. Vertigan saw them, and knew his friends were gone. Somewhere nearby the Oracle screamed his name.

Then the nothingness took him.

CHAPTER ONE

Homeward

'It was the Sylvaneth who healed me,'
Vertigan explained, leaning over the
side of the airship and gazing into
the tangled forest below. Strange cries
echoed from the twisted trees and
shimmering light danced in the depths.
'Without Litheroot I would've been lost.
Not dead, perhaps, like the others. But
gone, nonetheless.'

Kiri heard deep sadness in the old
man's voice, and his face was drawn
and weary. But at least now she
understood her purpose, the reason
she and her friends had been drawn
together. They had to return to the

Arbour, open the Soulspring and save the city of Lifestone, before it was overrun by the sorceress Ashnakh and her army of the dead.

Alish stood at the wheel, steadying the *Arbour Seed* as night winds buffeted the little airship. The others perched on the benches to either side, silently pondering everything Vertigan had told them. Scratch shivered, huddling close to Kaspar, while Thanis sat upright in the prow, gazing out into the night. Barely any time had passed since they'd toppled Ashnakh's tower and escaped from the Realm of Death. Already, Kiri knew, the sorceress would be recovering her strength and marshalling her forces.

'How did Aisha do it?' Elio asked. 'Who gave her the power?'

'It was Nagash,' Vertigan spat. 'The Great Necromancer, Aisha's true master. Like you she was born in Lifestone, the child of ordinary market traders. But her parents were taken when she

was very young, I could never discover
exactly how. She was left in the care
of an ageing relative, a petty conjuror,
little better than a woods witch. But
the old woman was a follower of
Nagash, and hoping to impress him
she took this chosen child under her
wing, giving her the secret name of
Ashnakh and raising her in the ways
of Death, encouraging her to use the
power of her birthmark. Their intention
was to corrupt the ritual, to poison the
Soulspring and allow Nagash to claim

the soul of Lifestone for himself. A great prize indeed.'

'But you stopped her,' Kiri said. 'You broke the spell.'

'I did.' Vertigan nodded. 'She wasn't the only one who'd been training in secret. I'd become fascinated by the arcane arts, and had begun to learn all I could about the life of a witch hunter. I had just enough willpower to resist her, but I was the only one who could. And it cost me greatly. The ritual left me prematurely aged – it took me years to recover. My friends all lost their lives, Aisha included. It was Nagash who brought her back, returning her spirit so she could complete her task, find the next generation of marked children and corrupt the ritual again. We are the only ones who can stop her.'

'Why didn't you tell us before?' Kiri asked. 'Why the secrecy?'

'Tradition,' Vertigan sighed. 'The truth was always hidden until the morning of the ritual. And I suppose I was afraid, too. Afraid that if you learned the truth too soon, if you realised how much danger you were in, you might be too scared to continue. I should've known better.'

There was a sudden screech in the dark, a blood-chilling cry echoing above the trees. They heard the thrum of wings and Kiri saw a hideous shape in the moonlight, a scaly, lizard-like form soaring on ragged pinions. Its black body was ridged with bony growths and its jaw was spiked with hideous fangs.

'That's a terrorgheist,' Elio said with a shudder. 'I saw a picture of one once and it scared the life out of me. I never wanted to see one for real.'

Thanis peered closer. 'There's someone riding on it,' she said in awe. A saddle was strapped to the creature's frame, a silver figure clasping the leather harness.

'General Bloodspeed,' Kaspar said. 'He's Ashnakh's messenger, she sent him to alert her troops and start the attack.'

The soulblight vampire had spotted them – Kiri saw his blue lips draw back over pointed teeth, his bone-white skin shining in the moonlight. Then he snapped the reins and the terrorgheist surged forward, its barbed tail lashing behind it.

'Sigmar's hammer, why didn't he attack us?' Alish asked. 'That thing could've smashed us out of the sky.'

'He's scared,' Thanis sneered. 'Seven against one. He's a coward.'

But Kaspar shook his head. 'Ashnakh ordered him not to hurt us, remember? She wants us in Lifestone. She wants us to carry out the ritual, so she can poison it again. So she and her dark master can steal the soul of the city.'

'So why are we doing it?' Elio asked. 'Why don't we just fly away, somewhere she can't find us?'

'Because that would doom Lifestone forever,' Vertigan told him. 'The city must be restored or it will fade utterly, and one of the jewels of Ghyran will fall into ruin.'

'So we need to make sure we're prepared,' Kiri said determinedly. 'When she comes for us, we have to be ready to fight back.'

'Remember what Litheroot told us,' Thanis put in. 'She said if we could find Aisha's childhood home, we might discover something that could help us. Some way to weaken her. Do you think that's true, Master Vertigan?'

The old man pursed his lips thoughtfully. 'I looked for the place myself, but I could never find it. I came to suspect that Aisha had... well, that she had *warned* the house to watch out for me. Left a charm that hid it from my sight. You might have more luck. But it's still one house in an entire city, where will you start looking?'

Elio sighed nervously. 'I'm supposed to ask my father to give us access to the Archives. But you know, he might not help us. The last time we spoke it didn't go so well. He told me I wasn't his son any more.'

'But you've changed,' Kiri told him. 'Maybe he has too. And anyway, I'll come with you. To help persuade him.'

Elio's eyes narrowed. 'Don't shoot him with your catapult or anything will you?'

'I'll come too,' Kaspar said. 'I know Ashnakh best, if we're looking for something that connects to her, I might be able to spot it.'

'So what about the rest of us?' Thanis asked. 'Do you think we should all go?'

Vertigan shook his head. 'Someone must go to the Arbour and prepare for dawn,' he said, scanning the black horizon. 'I only hope we will have enough time.'

Beneath them the trees were beginning to thin out, and off in the distance Kiri could see the line of torches marking the outer walls of Lifestone. But between them and the city was a black gulf, the valley below dark and silent.

'Where's Ashnakh's army?' she whispered. 'Are they gone?'

No one spoke, and for a moment the only sound was the droning of the airship's aether-endrins. Then Thanis pointed and Kiri saw a moving speck, glittering silver as it soared from shadow into moonlight. The terrorgheist beat its wings, descending into the valley. And as it did so, a terrible cry went up.

The roar echoed from the steep slopes on either side, bellowing and howling and cursing in a hundred hideous tongues. Light bloomed below them, lines of sickly violet radiance erupting from the heart of the valley and spreading like vines. And everywhere it touched Kiri saw movement – corpse-warriors and skeletal steeds, soulblight regiments and shrouded banks of half-formed nighthaunts, all marching into position.

Bloodspeed landed his monstrous steed in the centre of the valley, torches flaring around him. He pointed one gloved hand towards the city and the dead army howled, turning to face the high shield walls of Lifestone. The earth shook as they started to advance, their feet pounding the dust, their siege engines groaning as they rolled over the stony ground.

'There's so many of them,' Thanis said in horror. 'The city'll be overrun long before daybreak.'

'My father and his Lifestone Defenders will be manning the walls,' Elio said. 'They'll give as good as they get.'

'No disrespect, but they're already outnumbered hundreds to one,' Kaspar pointed out. 'And that's before the rest of Ashnakh's forces arrive.'

Scratch whimpered and wrung his hands, but Kiri refused to be daunted. 'So we'll find a way to slow them down,' she said. 'I know the odds are against us, but they have been all along. And look how far we've come.'

'Kiri's right,' Vertigan said. 'What you've achieved is already miraculous. And I may have a way to stop this army in its tracks. It might not work, but if it does...' He frowned thoughtfully, gripping his staff.

They were approaching the city walls now, the ragged army churning and clamouring in the shadows below. 'Okay, Alish, take us down,' Kiri said, grabbing a rope and preparing to heave it over the side. 'As low as you dare.'

Alish twisted dials and pressure gauges, angling the airship towards the battlements. A phalanx of skeletal soldiers were already nearing the foot of the wall and Kiri saw siege ladders going up, rising in the spectral torchlight.

'Look for the fountain of Lifestone,' Elio said. 'That's my father's banner.'

More ladders rose from the dark, skeletal warriors clambering over the battlements and launching themselves at the Lifestone Defenders. But above the fray a bright flag flew, a silver fountain shimmering in the moonlight. Shouts sounded and Kiri saw a tall figure striding along the battlements, the torchlight gleaming on his bald head. Lord Elias drew a mighty broadsword and charged at the enemy.

Elio bit his lip. 'I'm not sure who I'm most scared of. A million walking skeletons, or him.'

Kiri laughed, tossing down the rope. 'I'll back you up,' she promised. 'Alish, keep the ship steady.'

Kiri climbed over the railing, descending hand over hand towards the battlements. Elio came next, but as Kaspar made to follow Thanis took his arm.

'Be careful,' she said. 'This time you won't have me around to catch you.'

He smiled ruefully. 'We'll be back before dawn,' he told her. 'That's a promise.'

Then he swung his leg over and began to climb down.

CHAPTER TWO

The Siege of Lifestone

Kiri watched as the *Arbour Seed* soared
away, arrows whistling from the dark
and thudding into its wooden hull.
Around her the night was lit with ten
thousand torches, burning bright gold
within the city walls and deathly violet
without. The army of the dead surged
against the barricades, breaking like
a wild, dark wave. The noise of their
advance was deafening.

'Come on,' Kiri shouted to the others,
drawing her catapult and starting
along the battlements. Kaspar tugged
a pikestaff from a twitching, skeletal
hand while Elio lifted a blazing lantern

from its hook, raising it in front of him
as they ran along the narrow stone
walkway.

A siege ladder slammed into the
parapet beside Kiri, hooked steel
pinions gripping the wall. She just
had time to load her catapult before
a skeletal warrior sprang over, a rusty
blade clutched in its bony grip. It saw
her and lunged, reeling backwards when
Kiri's close-range shot blew its skull to
powder.

Kaspar and Elio took hold of the

ladder, struggling to raise the heavy pinions. Another pair of corpse soldiers followed, but Kiri finished one with a catapult shot then shoved the second hard in the chest, sending it tumbling down into the courtyard. The ladder was thrown back and Kiri hoisted herself up onto the battlements to watch it fall, groaning under the weight of fifty climbing skeletons and crushing many more when it slammed into the ground.

Then she lifted her gaze to watch the dead army approach, and immediately wished she hadn't. They filled the valley as far as she could see, tattered pennants flapping in the breeze, huge catapults and trebuchets lumbering towards the city. The skeletal soldiers seemed to move with a single purpose, a single mind almost, marching in perfect formation. Huge plumes of dust rose, lit from beneath by that sickening violet glow. And there were more troops arriving, she saw, marching up the track that led through the woods from the Realmgate at Rawdeep Mere.

'What can you see?' Elio asked, trying to peer over. But Kiri shook her head.

'Nothing worth worrying about,' she said, and dropped back down.

They ran again, keeping low as they sprinted towards Lord Elias in the thick of the fighting. Three Lifestone Defenders battled alongside him, but as Kiri watched one of them fell to the undead, five skeletons swarming over the young soldier and dragging her off the wall. Kiri heard a crash from below, then silence.

'Father!' Elio shouted as the remaining warriors regrouped, sending skeleton after skeleton tumbling from the walkway. 'Father, over here!'

Elias broke off in mid-swing, and almost dropped his sword in surprise. Two of the skeletons saw their chance and leapt forward, but the other Lifestone Defenders dived in to protect their lord, cutting the skeletons down before they could strike.

Now the way was clear and Lord Elias strode along the rampart, his face red with fury and disbelief. 'What in the name of Sigmar do you think you're doing?' he barked. 'This is a battle, Elio. It is no place for boys.'

'Father, I must talk to you,' Elio said, trying not to cower before the furious lord. 'We might be able to defeat this army, but you have to listen to us.'

His father's expression changed from anger to amazement. 'Have you lost your mind?' he demanded. 'And who are these gutter rats with you?'

'This is Kaspar and Kiri,' Elio explained. 'They're my friends.'

Kiri put out a hand but Lord Elias just looked at it in disgust before turning back to his son. 'Glad as I am that you've finally found some companions,' he said, 'I'm afraid this is not the time. I don't know why these... things are here or what they want, but we are the only ones standing in their way.'

'But we do know,' Elio told him. 'We know all about it, father. There's this sorceress, you see, she sent the Skaven to capture Master Vertigan–'

'The Shadowcaster?' Lord Elias said. 'So you're still in the thrall of that old wizard, are you? Still chasing fairy tales and sorcery? Well, you can tell that old charlatan... you can tell him...'

His voice trailed off, his eyes lifting from Elio and staring out along the battlements. Kiri saw a white mist rising, coiling in the chill air. The nighthaunts gathered on the walkway, their dark eyes glowing beneath their shadowed hoods, clasping scythes and swords in their cold, grasping fingers.

There was a clang as one of Elias's men dropped his sword, backing away. His companion joined him and they fled into the night, wailing in terror. The lord himself took a step back, the broadsword trembling in his grip. But Elio put a hand on his father's arm, fixing him with a firm stare.

'We'll handle this. We've faced these things before.'

Kaspar stepped forward, and the nighthaunts cackled as they drew in. Kiri gulped and reached for Elio's hand, standing firm as the hideous phantoms drew closer.

'Son, no,' Elias spluttered weakly. 'You can't.' But he made no move to stop Elio; his feet seemed rooted to the spot.

Kaspar waited until the nighthaunts were almost upon them, then he tugged back his sleeve, exposing the rune of Shyish. 'Begone!' he shouted. 'I command you.'

The nighthaunts wailed in surprise and fear, coiling together in a quivering mass of mist and smoke. Kaspar advanced another step, thrusting the mark at them. And with that the spectres broke, fleeing over the wall and away into the night.

Kaspar sagged, letting out a ragged breath. Kiri could see the strain on his face – using the power took a toll on him that she didn't fully understand, she was just grateful to him for saving their lives.

'That was... impossible,' Lord Elias said tremulously. 'How did... How could...'

'It's a *very* long story, father,' Elio told him.

The lord looked at him, shaking his head. 'You're not my son,' he said. Then before Elio could react, he took the boy's arm. 'I mean, you're not the same boy who walked away from me a year ago. You're different, Elio. When those things came you showed no fear, you... you *defended* me. I think you've even grown taller.'

Elio blushed. 'A lot has changed,' he admitted. 'And I promise, I'll tell you all about it. But for now, we need your help.'

Lord Elias gathered himself, nodding firmly. 'Tell me.'

'We're looking for a house,' Kiri explained. 'Somewhere in Lifestone.'

'A girl called Aisha Sand lived there,' Kaspar added.

'And it's vital that we find it before dawn,' Elio finished.

The lord scratched his head. 'And you say this information could help stop this army in its tracks? I don't know, Elio, this seems pretty far-fetched.'

'Please, father,' Elio repeated, looking up into the lord's doubtful face. 'Trust me, just this once.'

Lord Elias nodded, then he reached down and took something from around his neck, handing it to Elio. 'Show this to the Archivist,' he said. 'Tell him I said to give you whatever you need.'

Elio gulped, looking at his open palm. A silver seal lay there, shaped like a fountain, strung on a leather cord. 'The lord's seal,' he said in awe. 'Father, I can't–'

'Take it,' Elias insisted, reaching out to close Elio's hand. 'Find whatever you need to find, and save our city.'

Elio nodded slowly, and Kiri could see

the weight of responsibility settling on
his shoulders. 'We won't let you down,'
he promised.

Lord Elias smiled at his son. 'I know.'

Then there was a crash behind them
and Kiri spun, loading her catapult.
Another siege ladder had struck the
battlements, and a second beside it.
A third was thrown up, and over the
walls came a tide of skeletal soldiers,
their swords already drawn.

'Go!' Elias shouted, raising his blade.
'I'll hold them off.'

'You will try,' said a voice, and Kiri felt her heart stop.

A silver figure bounded over the ramparts, dropping to the walkway. Bloodspeed's armour was bright in the moonlight, his longsword slicing the air as he approached. His eyes fell on Kaspar and he smiled cruelly.

'The mistress's little apprentice,' he said. 'I knew we'd meet again.'

Kaspar scowled back. 'Better an apprentice than an errand boy.'

Bloodspeed growled. 'You will pay for that,' he hissed. 'I may not be allowed to kill you, but I can cause you and your friends a lot of pain.'

'You'll have to come through me,' Lord Elias snarled, gritting his teeth as he stepped forward. With his free hand he gestured to Elio, pointing to a set of steps leading down from the ramparts to the city. 'Go. I'll deal with this one.'

Bloodspeed bounded forward, his sword flashing like lightning. But Lord Elias countered, and sparks flew as their blades clashed.

'Father, no!' Elio cried. 'He's too quick.'

'I said, go!' Lord Elias barked, trying to force the soulblight back. 'I will not tell you again.'

Kiri took hold of Elio's wrist, pulling him towards the steps. 'Your father's right,' she said. 'We have a job to do, remember?'

Kaspar was already descending, his hooded figure swallowed by the shadows. Elio looked at Kiri, his face torn. Over his shoulder she could see Bloodspeed advancing, Elias shielding himself from a rain of blows. The lord was holding his ground, but for how long?

Then there was a shout nearby and a second slender figure appeared on the ramparts, followed swiftly by a third. The soulblights ran to the aid of their general, sweeping out their steel swords. Lord Elias saw them and quailed. But still he lowered his head, driving at the enemy with all his might. Kiri saw three swords slashing downward, heard the crunch and tear as his armour took the blows. There was a furious cry of defiance then she pulled Elio away, down the steep steps to the courtyard below.

Down here it was eerily quiet, the sounds of battle echoing indistinctly overhead. They ran across a cobbled square between empty market stalls, making for an open street on the far side. But as they reached it a shout went up, reverberating from the stone buildings. Cries of dismay from the Lifestone Defenders were answered by screams of victory from their opponents, as word spread along the battlements.

'The Lord of Lifestone has fallen!' men shouted. 'Elias is gone!'

Elio tried to turn back but Kiri refused to let him, shoving him on into the street.

'There's nothing you can do. And the only way to get justice is to stop Ashnakh.'

Elio staggered, his face streaming with tears. Then he seemed to remember something and opened his hand. The lord's seal lay there, shimmering silver.

'If he's gone...' he said, forcing the words out. 'If he's gone, that means...'

Kaspar nodded. 'It means you're the Lord of Lifestone.'

Elio shook his head. 'No, I don't, I can't possibly–'

'Worry about it later,' Kiri said as shouts rose behind them. 'For now, just run.'

CHAPTER THREE

The Mark of Azyr

The streets of Lifestone were a shadowy maze as the airship drifted over, rising towards the tumbledown palace on the hill. Alish twisted the altitude gauges, taking them over the outer wall of the Arbour with its stone figures standing guard, their arms interlocked. *The wall looks strong,* she thought. *But will it be enough?*

They soared over the eastern wing of the palace, descending towards the central courtyard. But as they dropped there was a shout from behind them, echoing through the valley. At the base of the slope those foul lights still burned, more of them than ever now. They seemed to be spilling over the wall, pouring into the city like water breaching a dam. Guttural voices howled in the dark and Vertigan tipped his head, his mouth tightening as he understood what they were saying.

'Lord Elias has fallen,' he told them. 'Elio's father is dead, and the dark army has entered the city.'

Thanis gasped. 'Poor Elio. But doesn't that mean there's no one left to stop them?'

Vertigan nodded. 'The Lifestone Defenders will keep fighting, but without their leader they will not hold for long. As Kiri said, we must find a way to slow Ashnakh's forces down, make time for the others to return before daybreak.'

Alish opened the valves and they landed in the courtyard with a bump and a scrape, steam hissing from the pipes. When it cleared she saw the dome of the Atheneum rising over them, a broken shadow in the moonlight. Scratch looked around in wonder at the white walls and slender spires, but to Alish the Arbour looked smaller somehow, old and ruined and falling to pieces.

Inside the Atheneum things were even worse – the petalled dome stood open to the sky, the tiled floor puddled with rainwater. On the shelves the books were soaked and swelling, and the calculations she'd scrawled on the walls had blurred and run.

Vertigan strode to his study but Alish and her friends lingered, looking at the hole in the floor where the Skaven had snatched their master and the old mooring ropes that had once held the *Arbour Seed* in place. A rolling boom sounded from the city, followed by another wave of cries.

'What are we going to do?' Alish wondered aloud. 'We can't just sit here.'

Thanis bit her lip. 'I reckon if we push that set of shelves up against the door there, and maybe get some planks to nail to the—'

'I don't mean rearranging the furniture,' Alish said. 'That won't be enough. You heard Vertigan, we need to slow the dead army down, give Kiri and the others time.'

'But that's what he's doing, isn't it?' Thanis asked, gesturing to the study door. 'What do you want us to do, go down there and fight them?'

Alish sighed bitterly. 'No, I just... There must be a way we can help.'

Thanis shook her head. 'You know me, I'm not great at coming up with clever plans. Put a Skaven in front of me and I'll hit it, but I don't... I'm not...' Her voice trailed off and she looked at the hole in the floor, scratching her head thoughtfully.

'What is it?' Alish asked. 'Have you thought of something?'

Thanis opened her mouth, but before she could speak there was a flash of light and they heard a cry of anger.

'Master Vertigan?' Alish said, crossing the hall with Scratch and Thanis on her heels. They stepped into the study to find him clutching his hand and cursing bitterly. There were scorch marks on his palm and a burned smell in the air.

'What happened?' Thanis asked. 'Did something go wrong?'

'No, I intended to set my hands on fire,' Vertigan snapped. Then he sighed wearily. 'I'm sorry, Thanis. I'm weak, Aisha has left me vulnerable just when I need to be strong. That army is coming for us and I'm afraid I won't be able to stop them.'

Alish shivered. 'If you're afraid, where does that leave us? There must be something we can do, some way we can help.'

Vertigan leaned on his staff. 'What I'm trying to accomplish takes focus and strength. More than I can currently summon.'

Scratch let out a squeak, waving his left arm. For a moment Alish didn't know what he was trying to say, then she saw him gesturing to the rune on his wrist.

'Of course,' she said. 'Our marks have power, don't they? We shared it between ourselves, maybe we can share it with you.'

Vertigan looked at her doubtfully. 'What do you mean? The six of you can join your birthmarks somehow?'

'Didn't you?' Thanis asked. 'When your group were together, didn't you link up like that?'

Vertigan shook his head. 'I don't think we knew it was possible. But then, we never confronted the kind of danger you have. The threat we were facing only revealed itself at the end, until then all we really did together was train and study.'

'So could it work?' Alish asked.

Vertigan hesitated. 'I'm not sure I like the idea of taking your power, not for such a perilous endeavour.'

'We don't mind,' Thanis said. 'Honest.'

'It's more like sharing than taking, anyway,' Alish told him.

Vertigan nodded grimly. 'I suppose we must all be prepared to take risks, if we are to defeat Ashnakh. Come this way.'

He hobbled back into the Atheneum, stopping beneath the dome. Overhead the stars shone cold and Alish heard more thunder as the dark army continued their advance.

With one hand Vertigan held his staff in front of him, while with the other he drew a knife from his belt. Suddenly he slashed downward, a swift, violent motion, and to Alish's astonishment the wooden staff seemed to move in his grip, as though evading Vertigan's strike. It writhed and twisted as he held it steady, carving a symbol just below the tip – a spearhead with a stroke across it, and beneath that a circle.

'The rune of Azyr,' Alish breathed. 'But you said no one could wield that mark, you said it was too powerful.'

'I have no choice,' Vertigan said, sheathing the blade and extending his hand. 'The Charm of Calling is our last chance. Now hold on to me, all of you.'

The rune of Ulgu blazed on his wrist as Alish took hold, the others joining her. Scratch shivered, looking up at Vertigan in fear and excitement as the energy flowed through them.

Their master closed his eyes, lifting the staff over his head. It seemed to be glowing from inside, as though a flame had been lit within the living wood. Alish felt the power channelling through her birthmark as Vertigan began to speak, muttering so low and so quick that she could barely make out the words. She heard the name Sigmar, and the words 'almighty warriors', but the rest was lost.

Then Vertigan himself began to glow, light pulsating beneath his skin, like the sun through closed eyelids. Alish felt heat beneath her hands and Scratch whimpered as the warmth grew, scalding like hot metal. The staff was consumed with energy, wreathing the wooden shaft and coursing down into Vertigan's arm, setting his hair on end and sparking on the buckles of his leather armour.

Then the light flared suddenly and Alish was thrown back, stumbling to her knees. Thanis and Scratch staggered too, and looking up in amazement Alish saw Vertigan rising, his feet leaving the ground as though he was being drawn up by the pillar of white light that blazed from the staff, its radiance piercing the sky like a beacon.

Alish reached to grab him but Vertigan had already risen too high, drifting up into the open dome. 'Come on,' she said, sprinting towards a platform by the wall, jumping onto it and unhooking the counterweights. Thanis and Scratch joined her as the platform rose, keeping level with Vertigan. His mouth was still moving, his eyes lightly closed as he rose to the level of the dome and stopped in mid-air, hanging from the staff and the beam of light erupting from it.

'How do we get him down?' Alish asked as they climbed onto the steel walkway beneath the dome.

Thanis shook her head. 'Maybe we don't. Maybe this is what's meant to happen.'

'But we can't just leave him hanging there,' Alish protested. 'Can we?'

'You can,' a voice whispered, and she looked up. Vertigan's eyes had flickered open, light sparking from his gleaming pupils. His lips were still moving, running over the same mystical incantations, but somehow his words to her had slipped through, as though he was speaking with two tongues at once.

'This is... right,' he managed, his voice somehow close and far away at the same time. 'The charm is working. I only hope we have enough time.'

'And what if we don't?' Alish asked. 'What if Kiri and the others get pinned down? What if Ashnakh's army comes and you're still like this?'

But Vertigan's eyes had closed, the power consuming him.

Alish wrung her hands, looking through the glass of the dome and down into the shadowed city. Buildings blazed in the lower quarters, and in the narrow streets dark things were moving.

'Our friends are down there,' she said.

'There has to be a way we can help them.'

'Well, I did have a sort of idea before,' Thanis admitted. 'But it's bad. Like, really bad. Plans aren't my specialty.'

'Say it anyway,' Alish told her.

Thanis peered down towards the floor of the Atheneum, that ragged hole standing out like the pupil in a huge eye. 'I'll tell you,' she said. 'But you have to promise you won't laugh. First off, do we still have that Light of Tick-Tock thingy?'

CHAPTER FOUR

The Living City

Kiri, Kaspar and Elio sprinted through winding alleys and along shadowy, high-sided streets, darting through moonlit squares where stone statues of Sigmar and Alarielle stood silent guard. Behind them, all was raging chaos as Ashnakh's army surged into the city, destroying everything in their path. The air was filled with shrieks, the smash and shatter as another shop was torn down, another temple set ablaze.

But above them on the higher slopes, nothing moved. The city sat hunched on the hillside as though waiting to be overwhelmed, as though there was nothing any of its inhabitants could do to turn back the dark tide. *We're the only ones,* Kiri thought. *The only ones who can save it.*

Then she saw a gleam in the air, right above the highest peak of the city. Was it coming from the Arbour? A shaft of white light streaked into the sky, and above it she saw a mass of dark cloud. What was happening up there?

'The Archive is this way.' Elio's voice distracted her and she looked down.

He's exhausted, she thought, *trying to hold himself together and not think about everything that happened back at the wall.* For now, it seemed to be working.

'It should be just around this...' He slowed, frowning in confusion. 'This isn't right. There should be a big old stables here, across from the Archive building.'

'Maybe we took a wrong turn,' Kaspar said, looking up and down the winding street. On the right was a building with curved sides, its windows boarded up.

'Wait, I know this place,' Kiri realised out loud. 'That's the old theatre where we all met the first time, where we saw Kreech. Elio, you weren't there, but Kaspar was.'

Kaspar squinted at the domed structure, ragged scraps of ancient billboards still plastered to the wall. 'I think you're right. We snuck in through that boarded-up window there, and out through a big door on the far side.'

Opposite the theatre a sheer-sided building stood tall against the sky, its windows like black eyes. Kiri saw it and shivered.

'That creepy old house was there too,' she remembered. 'I thought about hiding inside but it gave me the absolute frights.'

'We'll just have to double back,' Elio said. 'Retrace our steps and try again.'

They followed him to a crossroads and turned right, heading up the hill once more. Hearing a shout Kiri ducked, yanking Elio into a doorway. Kaspar raised his hood as three Lifestone Defenders hurtled past in disarray, their armour battered and their blades broken. Behind them came a horde of skeletal warriors, their jaws clacking as they ran. One of the Defenders nocked an arrow and fired over her shoulder, slicing the spine of an undead soldier and sending its skull rolling off down the street. But the rest were still gaining, and the Defenders looked exhausted as they rounded a corner and vanished into the night.

'Shouldn't we help them?' Elio asked. 'They're my father's soldiers. I mean, they're my soldiers. Shouldn't I do something?'

'The best thing we can do is find that house,' Kiri assured him. 'Then get back to the Arbour without getting ourselves killed.'

They took another corner, hurrying past a row of shuttered shops. The street wound to the right, and Elio's mouth fell open.

'No,' he said. 'No, I don't believe it.'

Ahead of them was the dome of the theatre, and across from it the dark house, tall and somehow watchful.

'It's impossible,' Kaspar protested. 'We can't be here again.'

'Yes, we can,' Kiri said, thoughts rushing through her head. 'In a weird way it makes sense, doesn't it? Remember what Vertigan told us. The city is a living thing, it has a soul and a mind. I think it's trying to communicate with us.'

She looked around at the moonlit street.

'It's actually happened to me before. The very first time I was brought to the Arbour I tried to run away, remember? But somehow I kept getting turned around, the streets kept bringing me back. Like the city didn't want me to leave. Haven't you ever felt anything like that?'

Kaspar hesitated, then he nodded. 'When I first met Vertigan. I set off from Bowerhome not really knowing where I was going, and the next thing I knew I was outside the Arbour, right by an open window. It was like it wanted me to go in.'

'I had it too,' Elio admitted. 'After I left my father's house for the last time. I'd barely left home when I was right at the Arbour gates. I thought I was just confused or upset, but now I don't know.'

'We know that the city chose us,' Kiri said. 'It used our marks to bring us together. Now I think it's trying to lead us again.'

'You think it wanted us to come here?' Kaspar asked. 'Why?'

'Because of that,' Kiri said, pointing at the tall, grim-faced house towering over them. 'I think that's the place we're looking for.'

Kaspar peered up at it. 'It feels... mean. Like it really doesn't like me.'

Elio shivered. 'When I look at it, I

feel like it's looking back. And all I want to do is run away.'

'Well that's unfortunate,' Kiri told him. 'Because I'm pretty sure we have to go inside.'

Alish hurried along the tunnel in darkness, the warm air stinking of rot and damp fur. Scratch had taken the lead; she could hear his footsteps on the hard-packed earth. Thanis brought up the rear, the Light of Teclis fading as they left the gnawhole behind. Just like last time, they'd used the mystical artefact to span the bridge from their realm into the Skaven warren. Now they had to hope the ratmen didn't tear them to pieces before they could carry out their plan.

'Are you sure that boy knows where he's going?' Thanis asked, catching up to Alish. 'Because I'm already lost.'

'Of course he does,' Alish told her. 'You're one of us now, aren't you, Scratch?'

But the boy didn't answer and Alish slowed, listening. All she could hear was the distant drip-drip of water, echoing in the dark.

'You sure about that?' Thanis asked as Alish reached into her pocket for one of the Bolts of Azyr she'd recovered from her workshop at the Arbour. She tossed it and the tiny projectile exploded, white light flooding the passage. Scratch crouched a short distance away, squinting and beckoning to them.

'You see?' Alish said, and Thanis gave a doubtful grumble.

Scratch clicked his tongue, hurrying them down the passage.

'You really know your way around, don't you?' Alish asked him. 'How long were you down here before we found you? Can you remember anything at all from before?'

Scratch paused in a small antechamber lit by a reddish crystal embedded in the ceiling. He scratched his head thoughtfully, as though considering Alish's question.

'You must have come from Lifestone originally, like we all did,' she said. 'Don't you remember your mum or your dad, or anything?'

A pained look came over Scratch's face and he shook his head rapidly.

'Don't make him think about it if he doesn't want to,' Thanis said. 'I can't imagine it was very nice, being kidnapped by Skaven.'

Alish bit her lip. 'You're right, I'm sorry. I just thought being back in Lifestone might have jogged something. But maybe it'll come later.'

Scratch grinned, showing his yellow teeth, and Alish knew she was forgiven. The boy headed for a passage that branched off the main way and they followed, pressing on into the dark. It wasn't long before they saw pale light gleaming on the walls of the tunnel, growing steadily brighter.

The passage opened out and Alish found herself looking down over a familiar landscape – the warren's vast central cavern. It was bigger than the entire city of Lifestone, lit from above by a huge white crystal sunk into the black rock.

But things had changed since they were last here. The workshops and forges had fallen silent, the steel cart-tracks were broken and disused. The paddocks that had once held herds of Deepearth Delvers were empty now, their fences flattened. In the centre of the cave the great spire of black volcanic rock still stood tall, but the mansion on its peak was a blackened ruin, the crystal above streaked with soot and ash. Worst of all was the silence hanging over everything – where once the cave had been crowded with Skaven all scurrying about their wicked business, now it was a lifeless shell, quiet as a tomb.

'Where did they go?' Thanis whispered. 'Ashnakh can't have killed them all, can she?'

Scratch shook his head, ducking down and pretending to cower.

'He thinks they're just hiding,' Alish interpreted. 'So how do we find Kreech?'

Scratch pondered for a moment, then he gestured to the hammer strapped to Alish's back. She unhooked it and handed it to him, as Scratch retrieved a piece of rusted metal from the rocky floor; it looked like an old Skaven breastplate. He struck the plate with the hammer and a dull sound rang out, echoing from the walls. He hit it again but still there was no response – the cavern was silent.

'Hey!' Alish shouted as loud as she could. 'Kreech, we've come to talk to you!'

Thanis banged her gloves together, stamping her booted feet. 'Come on, you hairy villain!' she shouted. 'It's us, we're back-back!'

Scratch grinned, banging his makeshift gong, and from deep below Alish heard a sound building – a scratching and a scraping, a chattering and a squealing. It grew in volume, making the floor tremble.

Then from a hundred different boreholes the Skaven came pouring, welling like rancid water from the rocks. They swarmed in from every side, streams becoming rivers, a great furry tide washing through the cavern. Alish gripped her hammer and Thanis planted her feet, Scratch ducking behind her as the filthy creatures drew closer.

There weren't nearly as many as there had been, Alish saw, and those that remained were somewhat pitiful-looking, wearing scraps of leather and clutching rusty blades. But there were still hundreds of them, even thousands – far too many to fight, if it came to it. They just had to hope Thanis's plan worked.

'Out-out of my way!' a thin voice cried, cutting through the din of stamping and snarling. 'Let me through-through, vermin!'

Kreech came scrambling over the heads of his pack, his wicked grin filled with broken fangs. His fur was ragged and one of his ears was missing, but he dropped to the ground and bounded forward, wrapping the dirty tatters of a violet gown around his shoulders.

'Oh, you made a bad-bad mistake coming back here, girl-things.'

Scratch stepped from Thanis's shadow and Kreech saw him. He hissed coldly.

'Traitor,' he seethed. 'Come to

73

gloat-gloat, have you? Come to die, yes-yes.'

'Wait!' Thanis said, holding up her gloved hands. 'We want to–'

But Kreech wasn't listening. He advanced on her, claws bared. Thanis tried to take a step back but he lashed with his tail, wrapping it twice around her neck and squeezing tight. Thanis was dragged off her feet, gasping for air as she crashed to the floor of the cave.

CHAPTER FIVE

The Playroom

Kiri found a narrow passageway that
ran along the side of the silent house,
and led the others into the empty yard
beyond. Kaspar could feel waves of
cold malice emanating from the place,
seeping through the very stones. In
the tangled garden stood a statue on a
granite plinth, a hooded figure holding
a sword and a long staff. Its face was
in shadow but somehow he knew it was
staring at him, sculpted eyes drilling
into his soul.

'Nagash,' he whispered. 'The
Necromancer.'

Elio shuddered. 'Well at least we know

this is the right place.'

The building rose over them, glass windows splintering the sinking moon. Kaspar tried to count the storeys but somehow he couldn't – it was as though the place kept growing and shrinking beneath his gaze. Kiri crossed to the rear door, taking the handle and turning it. She shoved it with her shoulder but it was locked tight.

'Let me,' Kaspar said, drawing out his lock-picks and crouching by the keyhole.

'Once we're inside, what should we look for?' Elio asked. 'What do you think Litheroot sent us to find?'

'I keep remembering something Ashnakh said,' Kaspar told them, feeling with his pick. 'She told me that if I wanted to become like her, I'd have to rid myself of all... what was it? *Sentimental attachments*. Anything I cared about. She was young when all this happened, so maybe we're looking for something a child might own. Something they'd feel attached to.'

'Like my beast book,' Elio said.

'Or my catapult,' Kiri suggested.

Kaspar smiled. 'Most kids have toys rather than weapons, but something like that.'

He felt the tumblers click and the door swung open, hinges groaning ominously. Beyond it was a tiled hallway with scorched black walls and doors on either side. Kaspar girded himself and stepped inside, but as he did so he saw a flash of light and felt his birthmark burn like ice.

He shut his eyes instinctively as a bright vision printed itself on the backs of his lids. He saw a girl, maybe four years old, passing through this very doorway, her eyes streaming with tears. There was someone with her – an elderly woman with a pinched face, gripping the child's wrist as she tried to pull away. The girl was clutching something to her chest but Kaspar couldn't make it out, her cloak was folded around it. Then he opened his eyes and the vision was gone.

'Are you all right?' Elio asked as Kaspar steadied himself against the door frame.

He nodded. 'I'm fine, I just... Never mind.'

They crept along the hallway, boards creaking underfoot. At the end was an arch of dark mahogany with shapes carved into the frame – twisted faces and mystical runes, too scorched and blackened to make out clearly. The room beyond was large and windowless, the only light filtering through holes in the ceiling. There was a stone structure in the centre, a bare altar of some kind, and on the walls the burn marks were thick and black.

'I think this is where the fire started,' he said.

'But there's nothing here,' Kiri pointed out. 'No furniture, no artefacts. Nothing childish. Maybe it all got burned up.'

'But look,' Elio said, pointing. 'What about up there?'

Across the room was a flight of steps, twisted and scorched but still intact. They made for them, Kiri taking hold of the banister and testing her weight. The stairs groaned, but held up.

They climbed as quietly as they could, the house silent around them. Kaspar could feel his birthmark tingling, those waves of dread still lapping at the shores of his mind. And when he reached the top step and placed his foot on the landing, he felt that burning sensation again as another vision streaked before his eyes.

It was the same girl, older now, and running. She seemed to pass right through him, hurrying towards an open doorway on the far side of the landing. There was a strange chime in the air, music playing somewhere close by. He knew that tune, he'd heard it before. There was something in the girl's hand and he looked down to see what it was. Three dead rats swung by their tails, dripping red.

Then Kiri touched his arm and he snapped back, gripping the banister. He pointed to the doorway, the one the girl had vanished through.

'Th– that way,' he managed.

She looked into his face, her mouth tight with concern. Then she crossed to the door, pushing it open, and Kaspar saw her face fall.

'What is it?' Elio asked, shrinking back. 'Something bad?'

Kiri shook her head. 'Take a look.'

Kaspar joined them in the doorway, peering inside. The windows were broken and shafts of moonlight bathed the room, reflected from mirrors and picture frames and ornate brass fittings. There was furniture in there too, a dresser and a chair and a bed with four posts. But they were almost hidden from view, because covering the room from end to end, piled in heaps everywhere Kaspar looked, was a mass of ragged toys.

He saw dolls and doll's houses, tin

lords and wind-up soldiers, carriages and carved animals, manticores and gryph-hounds, and a rocking horse with a wicked, toothy grin. The walls were lined with stuffed birds, ravens and night-owls and mountain hawks, and from a jack-in-the-box rose the life-sized figure of a jester, perched on a rusted spring. Kiri nudged it as she stepped inside and little bells rang dully, the grinning figure swaying back and forth.

'Well this is terrific,' Elio said. 'How are we meant to know which is the right one?'

Kaspar stood in the centre of the room, turning to look around him. 'I don't know. But I feel like I'll know it when I see it.'

Kiri picked up a wooden figure, carved like a soulblight vampire with tiny steel fangs. 'How about this?' she asked, but Kaspar shook his head. Elio presented him with a stuffed rat, perched upright and clutching a sword in mockery of the Skaven. Kaspar hesitated, remembering his vision, but then he frowned.

'I don't think so. It just doesn't feel like *her*, somehow.'

He turned as he heard a sound nearby, a dry rustling.

'What was that?' Elio asked, shrinking closer to Kiri as she drew her catapult.

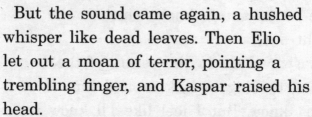

'I'm not sure,' Kaspar whispered. 'Maybe just the floor creaking.'

But the sound came again, a hushed whisper like dead leaves. Then Elio let out a moan of terror, pointing a trembling finger, and Kaspar raised his head.

On the wall was one of the stuffed ravens, its dark wings outstretched. But as Kaspar watched the wings started to flap, slowly at first then with more force. A strangled caw escaped its beak, and its glass eyes seemed to flicker with life.

Feeling movement against his leg, he looked down. Tiny hands were grasping his boots, clawing at the seam of his trousers. He kicked and saw a small porcelain doll fly off into a heap of toys. But the doll rolled over, glaring up at him through marble eyes, its cracked face grimacing. It clambered up and came for him again, scrambling over the piles of ragged playthings as they twitched and writhed and jerked into life.

Kiri yelled out as the armless jester lunged at her, steel teeth snapping as it swayed on its spring. Kaspar saw puppets breaking their strings and dropping to the floor, moving towards them with a sickening herky-jerky motion. The rocking horse began to totter wildly, letting out a hoarse bray like mad laughter. Lights flickered in the windows of the doll's houses, their tiny occupants streaming out and joining the fray.

The wind-up soldiers

formed ranks and began to charge, flinging themselves from the dresser and leaping onto Elio's coat, scrambling upward. He batted them away but they kept coming, making for his startled face. Kiri took out her catapult but they were too hemmed in, and she couldn't get a clear shot. So instead she tore the leg from one of the larger dolls, wielding it like a club to drive the others back.

'We have to go!' she yelled at Kaspar. 'I can't hold them off!'

'But we haven't found it yet,' he shouted back. 'This could be our only chance.'

He looked around desperately as the toys swarmed in from every side. But none of them felt right – they were all too gaudy, too colourful, not serious enough for a girl like Aisha. A woolly basilisk had wrapped around his thigh, biting him with fluffy fangs, while a carved gryphon butted at him with both its heads, trying to knock him off balance. He stumbled, grabbing the bedpost, and that's when he saw it.

This time the vision overwhelmed him utterly, his birthmark blazing. He saw the girl jumping up off the bed, crossing to a mirror over the fireplace. That music was in the air again, and this time he recognised it – he'd heard it in the Castle of Mirrors, first in his dreams, then in the stairway. And he knew it from before, too, from somewhere deep in his memory.

The girl inspected herself in the mirror, and now he could see her face clearly for the first time. Aisha Sand was beautiful even then – but beneath her pale skin he could see Ashnakh, waiting to be born. Then their eyes met in the mirror and the girl gasped, turning. As she did so she knocked something with her hand, sending it crashing to the floor.

The music stopped dead and Kaspar opened his eyes. He knew what he was looking for.

The toys clawed at him as he shoved forward, forging a path. He reached the fireplace, the cracked mirror shattering his reflection into a thousand pieces. Then he bent down and felt with his hands, ignoring the pain as a tin soldier jabbed a sword into his thumb.

'Come on!' Elio cried, his voice muffled. 'What are you doing?'

But Kaspar barely heard him, clutching at an object that lay upended, its lid open. He tugged it free, kicking back towards the door as wings beat and hands grasped, trying to pull him down. He clasped the music box to his chest and ran for the stairs, shoving Kiri and Elio ahead of him.

Thanis clawed at the fleshy tendril wrapped around her neck, her face turning

86

a hideous shade of red. Scratch tugged at his former master, pulling Kreech's cloak and whining. But the packlord shook him off, knocking the boy down in the dirt.

Alish was frozen in fear, watching as Thanis struggled and fought. It had all happened so fast, she wasn't prepared, not for this. There were so many of them, all pressing in around her, how could she possibly hope to fight?

Then a thought struck her and she broke from her daze, scrabbling desperately in her pocket. She threw the Bolt of Azyr down on the stones in front of Kreech, sending wild shadows leaping around the cavern. The ratmen drew back, hissing fearfully, but Kreech stood his ground, his tail tightening.

'Cowards, it's only flash-flash!' he told his underlings. 'Grab the other girl-thing.'

Alish retreated, drawing her hammer and preparing to swing. But Scratch leapt in front of her, waving frantically, something clasped in his hand. The packlord saw it and his eyes widened.

It was a small cloth sack tied with thread, just like the one Kreech wore at his belt. The packlord reached down, patting his waist in disbelief as Scratch tore the pouch open, tipping the contents into his hand.

A violet glow lit up his face, crystals sparkling in his open palm. Kreech's jaw dropped, his tail slackening, allowing Thanis to draw breath.

'Give-give,' Kreech said, beckoning to Scratch. 'Now, my pet.'

But Scratch shook his head, taking a step back. He pointed to the warpstone then up into the air, miming a large, mounded shape. He spread his arms wider and wider, indicating something huge.

'Warpstone?' Kreech asked dubiously. 'Lots-lots of warpstone?'

Scratch nodded fiercely, then he pointed to Thanis and shook his head. Kreech frowned uncertainly, but he uncoiled his tail nonetheless. The girl dropped to all fours in front of Alish, hacking and coughing.

'My boy-pet says you have warpstone,' Kreech growled. 'A lot of it.'

'It's true,' Alish told him. 'More than you can imagine. A whole mountain of it.'

Thanis staggered to her feet.

'We can... we can show you. It's magnificent.'

Kreech's eyes lost focus, a trickle of drool running through the gaps in his teeth and down onto his robe. Then he snapped back, shaking his furry head.

'Why should I trust-trust you?' he demanded. 'You broke my prize. You burned my beloved manse-home. You released my beautiful delvers, yes-yes.'

'Why else would we dare come back here?' Thanis asked. 'We'd only take such a risk if we had something to offer you, something you couldn't refuse.'

'Ashnakh kept this warpstone secret from you,' Alish added. 'The piece she gave you was less than a crumb.'

The packlord hissed. 'The mistress must pay-pay for what she did to Kreech. Her dead-things beat him and hurt him so. She swore to return, to finish Kreech herself, but she never came.'

'Well, we've been keeping her pretty busy,' Thanis said.

Alish faced Kreech. 'How would you like to deal with Ashnakh before she can deal with you? How would you like to be rich again, and respected?'

Kreech snarled sceptically. 'And I suppose there is something you want, girl-things? Some task I must perform before I gain this impossible prize?'

'Of course,' Thanis told him. 'But for a powerful Skaven like you, it should be easy.'

'It'll mean defying Ashnakh openly,' Alish said. 'It'll mean stopping the mistress in her tracks. And it'll mean causing all kinds of mayhem.'

Kreech cackled, his eyes glittering in

the gloom. 'Oh, girl-things. We Skaven
are the masters of mayhem, yes-yes.'

CHAPTER SIX

The Dead Army

Kiri held on to Kaspar's arm, supporting him as they burst through the back door and into the moonlit courtyard. He was clutching something in his hands, a box of some sort, gripping it like a drowning man as they hurried around the side of the house and back into the silent street.

Below them the city was ablaze, pillars of flame billowing above the torchlit outer wall. The battle still raged, the night split by the clash of steel. The higher slopes were still in darkness but above the Arbour that strange light flickered, illuminating a dense swirl of dark cloud that circled overhead. That was odd, Kiri thought. Earlier the skies had been clear. She felt a chill breeze and a sudden feeling of familiarity flooded over her, like she'd been here before – the clouds, the wind, that unearthly light.

'Did you get what we came for?' Elio asked Kaspar. 'Are you sure?'

Kaspar clasped the box tighter. 'I'm sure.'

'Then let's move,' Kiri said, starting up the street, glad to leave Aisha's home behind them. 'We'll head for the Arbour, find the others, and hope Ashnakh's army don't–'

She broke off, skidding to a halt. Just ahead the winding street opened into a large stone square, enclosed by shuttered buildings on all four sides. And filling the square from end to end, their skulls pale in the dim light, were ranks of skeletal soldiers.

'Back,' Kiri hissed to the others, gesturing frantically. 'Quickly.'

'Careful now,' a voice said behind them. 'You don't want to take a wrong turn.'

Kiri turned, and her throat tightened. Up the street came another column of undead warriors, their bony feet tramping on the cobblestones. And at their head strode a familiar figure, his silver armour sparkling in the torchlight.

'We meet again,' Bloodspeed said. He smiled. 'I knew we would.'

Elio snarled, starting forward, but Kiri held him back. 'You murdered my father,' he managed, his voice thick with anger. 'You'll pay for that.'

Bloodspeed smiled thinly. 'The old man fought hard, I'll admit. But he was weak.'

'He was the Lord of Lifestone,' Elio spat. 'And now that honour has fallen to me.'

Bloodspeed nodded. 'You're brave, lordling. But it won't save you.' His attention turned to Kaspar and he beckoned with one gloved finger. 'Come, little apprentice. The mistress is eager to see you. I'm to take you and your friends to her, then we'll all go up to that Arbour of yours.'

Kaspar laughed. 'Not a chance. If she wants us, tell her to come herself.'

Kiri loaded her catapult, knowing it was no use. There were a hundred skeletons advancing up the street and many times more in the square behind them.

'Leave us alone,' she said. 'Or I promise, you will suffer the consequences.'

Bloodspeed sneered. 'And who are you, then? Another lost child?'

'Not any more,' Kiri told him. 'This city is my home, and I'll fight to the death to defend it.'

She let fly and the shot struck Bloodspeed's breastplate with a clang, denting the filigreed silver. He seethed, inspecting the damage. Then he started forward, unsheathing his sword. Kiri backed up, the others beside her. But there was nowhere for them to go – the skeletal soldiers filled the square, boxing them in.

Then suddenly the earth shook, a tremor that seemed to pass up the sloping street and out across the square. Bloodspeed looked down in confusion as the earth rumbled beneath him, and several of the skeletons lost their balance.

'What trickery is this?' the soulblight demanded. 'What fresh deception have you foul children come up with now?'

The groaning grew louder, cracking and creaking, and Kiri clutched Elio as the stones vibrated beneath them. The buildings rattled, clouds of dust billowing from the ground. For a moment Kiri felt her birthmark tingling.

Then Kaspar cried 'Get back!' and Kiri threw herself clear as the stone square split open down the middle, a huge crack widening rapidly. Paving slabs were flung violently into the air, crashing down and crushing skeletal soldiers. Many more toppled into the sudden breach that had appeared before them.

There was a deep tearing sound like a thousand claws scrabbling the earth, and as the ground rocked again Kiri heard screeching and clamouring, a savage din that grew in volume until it resounded from every wall of the square. The rift down the centre split wider, stones and skeletons toppling inside. She looked down and saw eyes in the dark, hundreds of them, too many to count, all rushing towards her.

The Skaven erupted from the earth, welling like black lava. Their claws and teeth were bared and many carried blunt swords and axes, shaking the dust from their pelts as they sprang into the square.

'Fight-bite!' a voice cried from below. 'Attack, my Skaven!'

The ratmen fell on the skeletal army,

gnawing and biting and slashing. Kiri
saw skulls and leg-bones flying loose,
arms spinning through the air as the
Skaven drove mercilessly forward. She
kept close to Kaspar and Elio; the
Skaven might be attacking their enemy,
but she doubted they'd make much
distinction between the dead warriors
and three man-thing children.

'Form up!' a voice barked from the far
side of the square. 'Fight back, curse
you!'

General Bloodspeed watched in dismay

as the ratmen swept through his ranks, ripping his soldiers to pieces. Then his eyes fell on Kiri and she saw his lip curl. He pointed a steel-gloved finger at her, then he drew it across his throat.

The soulblight backed up several paces, eyeing the chasm that lay between himself and his prey, ragged Skaven still leaping from it. Then he put his head down and ran, his boots pounding on the stones. Kiri snatched for her catapult, loosing a shot, but it had no effect, ricocheting uselessly off the general's armour.

Bloodspeed reached the edge of the chasm and sprang, vaulting over the heads of the Skaven, his eyes red with bloodlust. But midway through his leap something flew from the chasm, a tiny object spiralling towards him. Bloodspeed just had time to notice it before the Bolt of Azyr exploded, letting out a flash of dazzling light.

The general bellowed, recoiling as the light burned his sensitive vampire eyes.

He was thrown off balance, crashing to the ground, his silver armour twisted.

He tried to pick himself up but something had hold of him, claws seizing at his legs, his hands, his hair. The Skaven swarmed over him, snapping and screeching, tugging him over the edge of the chasm and down into the dark. The last Kiri saw of him was a desperate, outstretched hand. Then he was gone.

'Didn't that silver fool learn *anything* from last time?' a voice echoed from the pit. 'You don't mess with the chosen of Lifestone.'

Kiri watched in amazement as a tall figure clambered from the crevasse, scrambling up into the moonlight. Thanis turned to help Alish and Scratch, then she looked around at the battle still raging, the Skaven and the skeletons tearing at one another. Alish was the first to spot Kiri, her face lighting up.

'It was all Thanis's idea,' she said

as Kiri raced over, pulling Alish in for a hug. 'Scratch led us through the warren. But it was me who threw that Bolt of Azyr.'

'It was perfect,' Kiri said. 'But how did you... Where did they all...'

'Your friends made a bargain,' a sneering voice answered. 'And now they must keep-keep it.'

Kreech bounded from the pit, his tattered cloak around his shoulders. Behind him the Skaven were still fighting, but the packlord had eyes only for Kiri and her friends.

'My warriors have done as you asked,' he said to Thanis. 'We will rip-tear the streets and slow-slow the mistress's bone-men. Now where is this outrageous warpstone you promised me?'

Thanis winced awkwardly, then she turned and pointed out into the night, beyond the buildings, beyond the city walls where the army were still streaming in. 'It's about... twenty leagues that way,' she said. 'Deep in the forest there's a dry lake, it's called Rawdeep Mere. The warpstone is at the bottom of it.'

Kreech bared his teeth. 'Twenty leagues? At the bottom of a lake? You swore-swore to me, you promised warpstone. You said it would be mine!'

'We said we'd tell you where it was,' Alish reminded him. 'And we have.'

'And anyway,' Thanis added, 'we knew that as soon as we told you, you'd turn on us. Now there are more of us, and your Skaven are busy with Ashnakh's army.'

Kreech growled deep in his throat, but it soon turned to cold, hacking laughter. 'You know me too well, girl-thing. That's almost devious enough for a Skaven. I will claim my prize, be sure of that. But I will deal with you first.'

He gestured with his claw and a number of ratmen peeled off from the fight, scurrying towards him. 'See how they obey me?' the packlord said with a smirk. 'You will learn to do the same, little man-things. A few days, weeks-weeks, years working to rebuild my beautiful warren, and you will be my slaves, yes-yes.'

'I'm nobody's slave!' Kiri aimed her catapult but the ratmen sprang, one seizing her wrist and yanking it down. Kaspar rushed to help her but a second Skaven was already on him, a third taking hold of Thanis. More came bounding in, and Kiri felt Elio's panicked breath on her neck as they were forced together, sealed in a wall of pulsating fur.

'I wonder, which shall I punish first?' Kreech snickered. 'The girl-thing who freed my beautiful delvers? The little lordling who tried to trick-trick me? Or my own treacherous little pet?' He glanced from Kiri to Elio to Scratch, before his eyes fell on Kaspar. 'Of course. The boy-thing who broke my beautiful prize. I'll start with–'

There was a boom and a flash of light, stinging Kiri's eyes. The Skaven howled and she smelled singed fur, something crashing into her and tumbling past.

When her vision cleared she saw Kreech lying on his back, his claws swiping at the air, smoke rising from his blackened belly. On the stones around him was a circular blast mark where a fire-bolt had struck the ground.

There was a rumble of thunder and the Skaven shrank, cowering and covering their faces. Kiri looked up and saw a figure silhouetted against the

churning clouds.

Ashnakh was wreathed in violet energy, wraiths coiling around her as she formed another skull-headed fire-bolt and prepared to let loose. Kreech looked at her and wailed.

CHAPTER SEVEN

Lightning

Kreech stumbled to his feet as the sorceress descended between the buildings, her hands coiling. He tried to flee but Ashnakh loosed a second fire-bolt and he was tossed like a leaf, thrown head over claws to the edge of the chasm. He clung there, scrabbling desperately, then he dropped out of sight.

Thanis tugged at Kiri's sleeve. 'Come on, while she's distracted.'

Alish and the others were already moving, heading for the top of the square where a row of houses had slumped into the crevasse, forming a rough bridge. They clambered over loose bricks, sending rocks and dust sliding into the chasm. But as Kiri reached the top she dared a glance back, to see Ashnakh land light-footed on the stones. Skeletons and Skaven stood watching in silence, the battle forgotten.

Elio pointed to an alley nearby. 'This way,' he said. 'If Ashnakh comes after us maybe we can lose her in the backstreets.'

Kiri followed, Thanis and Scratch close behind. Kaspar brought up the rear, but before he'd taken three steps something snaked from the pit and lashed around his ankle, dragging him off his feet. Kaspar cried out, rolling over as Kreech rose from the crevasse, his fur black and smoking, his blistered tail yanking Kaspar backwards.

'Not so fast, sneak-thing!' the packlord hissed, baring his claws. 'I will have my rev– aaagh!'

The words choked in Kreech's throat, his eyes widening in fear. His tail was still tight around Kaspar's ankle but across the crevasse Kiri could see Ashnakh turning towards him, one hand raised as waves of dark power filled the air. Kreech tried to lift his head but he was pinned in place, gasping for breath as the sorceress tightened her invisible grip.

'I told you, treacherous creature,' she said, her soft voice echoing. 'I want those children alive. But the same is not true for you.'

There was a creaking, cracking sound and Kiri looked down. Kreech's feet had become rooted to the ground, his clawed hands rigid in the air. A gurgling hiss escaped the packlord's throat but he could not speak – his jaw was frozen.

His fur began to change colour, just the roots at first then the tips too, spreading like violet hoar frost. His eyes misted over, the black pupils turning purple along with his claws and his teeth. Kiri heard a groan like ice on a frozen lake, and Kreech let out a last, strangled breath as his body froze solid.

Then Ashnakh's head tipped and she smiled briefly. Her hands coiled and she loosed another fire-bolt, the skull at its heart screaming as it came. Kaspar kicked, and Kreech's tail shattered as he broke free. Then the fire-bolt struck the rigid Skaven and he exploded into a thousand shards, scattering like glass into the air.

Not glass, Kiri realised, *warpstone.* She had transformed him into warpstone.

The other Skaven watched as their master disintegrated, pieces of him flying everywhere. Then slowly, the fear in their eyes turned to something else. Hunger.

The first Skaven broke from its stupor, snatching up a piece of the purple crystal and jamming it into its jaws. Another followed, and another, then the ratmen were all clamouring wildly in their direction, seizing and consuming whatever fragments of their former packlord they could find. Kiri turned away, feeling sick to her stomach.

'Let's go,' Elio hissed, turning for the alleyway.

But Ashnakh hadn't forgotten them. The sorceress made a gesture and Kiri felt her muscles respond, felt that horribly familiar sense of someone taking over her body. For a moment she was terrified, remembering what had happened to Kreech.

No, she remembered. *Ashnakh needs us.*

The others were caught too, turning jerkily as Ashnakh twisted her hand. 'Please, don't leave,' the sorceress said. 'There's no need now, is there? We all want the same thing. To carry out the ritual.'

She beckoned and Kiri was forced to the lip of the crevasse, warpstone crunching underfoot. Her friends joined her, stepping in unison, caught in Ashnakh's spell. The sorceress laughed,

a cold, delighted sound, then she
tipped her hand from side to side like
a puppeteer. Kiri felt her body twitch,
jerking first left then right, her arms
swinging at her sides. She tried to
break free, to reach for Thanis, but
somehow Ashnakh's power had grown
stronger, harder, more vicious.

'What fun,' the sorceress said, raising
and lowering her hand so that all six
of them stretched up on their tiptoes
then slumped back down. 'I wonder
what else I could make you do? Jump

into this pit? Attack one another? No, no, we have a task before us, don't we?'

As she rambled on, a cold certainty filled Kiri. Destroying her Castle of Mirrors hadn't just dealt a blow to Ashnakh's plans. It seemed to have affected her mind, too. The person facing them now wasn't the same one they'd escaped back in Shyish – Ashnakh's eyes were brighter, her smile wider. They were in the grip of a madwoman.

'It'll be easier if you don't fight,' she cackled. 'We can all go together, back up to that old ruin. We'll find your master and then it'll be time for the–'

There was a rumble of thunder, loud and sudden, ricocheting from the buildings around the square. Ashnakh frowned, glancing up into the sky. Helplessly, Kiri did the same, her neck jerking upwards. Once again she saw black clouds, churning like a whirlpool. They moved restlessly, the eye of the storm poised directly over the city.

Then a cold wind blew, gusting through the square, and she noticed how quiet it had become. The Skaven and the skeletal soldiers stood gazing upward, some of the ratmen whimpering softly. In the centre stood Ashnakh, her face tight with concern.

Gathering her strength, Kiri *pushed* as hard as she could. Her hand began to move, slowly at first, reaching towards Thanis at her side. She kept pushing, kept forcing herself, snagging with the tips of her fingers at Thanis's sleeve. Ashnakh tore her eyes from the sky, but by then it was too late.

Kiri's fingers locked around Thanis's wrist and immediately she felt the power of their marks surging through her. She *shoved* with her free hand, reaching for Elio as Ashnakh flung out her hands, trying to regain control. But Elio and Thanis reached for Scratch and Alish, who in turn took hold of Kaspar, clutching his hand tightly. The six of them stood in a ragged line before the sorceress, power surging through them.

Ashnakh cursed and Kiri saw another fire-bolt within her coiled hands, sparks lighting her wild, unfocused eyes. Then the sorceress lashed out and Kiri reacted instinctively, throwing up her hands to shield herself from the impact. But instead there was a clap of thunder, so loud it made her ears ring. Lightning sliced from the clouds, a jagged bolt skewering Ashnakh's fire-bolt and tearing it to pieces.

Kiri blinked in disbelief. There on the stones stood a warrior with a fork of lightning emblazoned on his helmet, grasping a silver sword and a huge steel hammer. His armour gleamed gold and deep blue, and above his helmet rose a spiked crown.

'A Stormcast Eternal,' Kiri whispered in awe. 'They've come.'

She had seen the fabled warriors of Sigmar in action once before, and it was a sight she would never forget. Legend told that the Stormcasts had once been mortal, before they were chosen by the lightning and reforged in the fires of Azyr, given strength and courage far beyond that of any ordinary soldier. Now they were the front-line troops in the struggle against Chaos, riding the storm into the heart of battle, wherever their might was needed most.

Another bolt struck the cobbled square, and another. Each revealed a golden warrior, standing upright and determined. Ashnakh faced them, her face twisted with dismay. She made a sweeping gesture and her skeletons turned as one, advancing on the Stormcasts.

'Fight them,' she commanded. 'Kill them!'

The Skaven regarded the new threat, chattering and bickering amongst themselves. Then they reached a decision and began to swarm forward, approaching the Stormcasts from all sides.

Kiri saw lightning striking left and
right, Stormcasts emerging all across
the square. But the Skaven and the
skeletons were many, falling on the
golden figures with swords and teeth
and claws. The first Stormcast swung
his hammer and Kiri saw fur flying,
bones scattering, and heard the wail of
Skaven. But there were already more
running to take their place, and more
behind those.

The storm rolled overhead, lit with
flashes of lightning. But looking up she

noticed that the light from the Arbour was gone, replaced by a different kind of radiance, a pale gleam above the peaks of the mountains.

'The sun's coming up,' Kaspar said. 'We're running out of time.'

'So what are we waiting for?' Thanis asked as another bolt of lightning struck, another Stormcast wading into the fray. 'I think this lot can look after themselves.'

Elio took the lead, sprinting into the narrow alleyways of Lifestone. Kiri and Kaspar were right behind him, followed by Alish holding Scratch by the hand. Thanis brought up the rear, grabbing a loose stone from the ground and hefting it.

The alley twisted left and right, branching and diverting, always in the shadow of tall buildings. As they crossed wider streets they saw knots of fighting – Skaven and skeletons, Stormcasts and soulblights, even a squad of Lifestone Defenders, battling ferociously as the corpse legions pinned them down. Silently Kiri begged the city to help them, to work its magic and lead them swiftly to the Arbour. Her hopes rose when the alley straightened out and she saw the white towers of the palace rising ahead, behind the wall of grey granite figures standing arm in arm.

'They're Stormcasts,' Alish realised aloud, hurrying beside Kiri. 'That's what they're meant to look like, isn't it? A wall of guardians, defending the Arbour.'

Kiri nodded, remembering the light she'd seen in the sky earlier, those flashes from the Arbour. Had Vertigan called these warriors down? For a moment she felt almost hopeful – surely the Stormcasts could turn the battle's tide. But then the alley opened and she saw the wide stone road surrounding the Arbour, and her heart seized.

An entire legion of skeletal soldiers

had arrived ahead of them, erecting
ladders and wooden scaffolds, laying
siege to the palace. A mob of Skaven
had attacked them, tearing the street
to shreds as they clawed their way up
from the ground. But now a phalanx of
Stormcasts had arrived too, the golden
soldiers advancing in a deadly line,
trying to drive the ratmen back. The
Skaven surged against the Stormcasts,
clawing over one another in great
waves. And to Kiri's horror some of
the golden warriors were borne down,
swords flailing as the Skaven took hold.

'Wait,' Thanis said in shock. 'I thought
Stormcast Eternals were invincible.'

Kiri shook her head. 'No one's

invincible,' she said as the golden warriors fought to their feet, flinging startled Skaven every which way. 'But they are very, very tough.'

The Stormcasts drove the Skaven back and now the street ahead was clear. Above the dome of the Atheneum the sky was growing pale, shafts of sunlight brushing the clouds.

They ran, dodging past a pair of shuffling skeletons, Kiri using her catapult to take down a leaping Skaven. As they reached the rusted steel gates she turned for a last look across the beleaguered city, where billowing clouds of smoke still blackened the morning air. Everywhere she looked she could

see fighting – down by the wall, in the market and the streets, around the warehouses at the base of the slope and among the mansions at its heights. And she knew that today would either mark the salvation of this great city, or its ultimate destruction.

CHAPTER EIGHT

The Ritual

Vertigan was waiting for them in the
doorway of the Arbour, his face heavy
with exhaustion. Scratch followed
his friends up the stone steps, his
head still spinning from all that
had happened. He knew something
important was about to occur, something
that would change his life forever. He
was terrified, but it was exciting too.

Vertigan faced Kaspar. 'You found
what you were looking for? Show me.'

The boy hesitated then held out a
varnished wooden box, its lid firmly
closed. 'I don't know what good it'll
do, but I'm sure this is what Litheroot

meant us to find.'

Vertigan took it, running a hand over the smooth surface. 'Strange. I was expecting it to contain some powerful force, some ancient evil. But all I feel is... innocence.'

He shook his head thoughtfully then started back into the palace, leading them along a rubble-strewn corridor with a high ceiling and flaking pictures on the walls. Scratch saw warriors with bright swords and flashing eyes, and terrible beasts with wings and teeth and fire coming out of their mouths. He clung close to Alish as they ran, hearing a rumble outside and seeing a flash light up the crumbling corridor.

'Did you summon the Stormcast Eternals?' Thanis asked. 'Is that what the mark of Azyr was for?'

Vertigan nodded. 'I wasn't sure whether Sigmar would answer my call,' he said. 'Luckily, his warriors arrived just in time. I didn't even think of allying with the Skaven, however. That was a risky strategy, but a shrewd one.'

The tall girl blushed as red as her hair. 'No one ever called me shrewd before.'

'Was it enough, though?' Kiri asked. 'Have the Skaven and the Stormcasts bought us enough time to carry out the ritual?' Pale light was already filtering through the windows on both sides of the hallway as dawn spread across the sky.

'We can only try,' Vertigan told them, pausing before a set of glass doors. 'But I believe in you. All of you.' He ruffled Scratch's hair and the boy beamed up at him.

Then he pushed open the doors and strode into the courtyard, where dry leaves blew in the morning wind and the shadows of bare trees slanted over the dead ground. On the far side Scratch could see the airship that had brought them here, and that had been his home for those few days back in Shyish. The thought of that evil place reminded him of the sorceress that had pursued them, and he wondered how long it would be before she caught up. Hopefully those golden soldiers were keeping her busy.

In the centre of the courtyard stood a tall shape, a drystone spire carved with the heads of monsters, with a marble bowl bulging from its middle. Scratch felt the mark on his wrist tingle as they approached, and shivered with anticipation.

He didn't need to look for his place at the fountain – the rune of Ghur called to him, a fletched arrow carved deep into the lip of the bowl. The others stood in a circle around him, each finding their own symbol etched in the stone. Vertigan took his place across from Scratch, silhouetted by the sun as it rose behind the mountains. The old man's eyes were filled with pride, but there was weariness there too, and worry.

'It won't be like it was before,' Kaspar

assured him, standing beside Scratch. 'We won't let you down like Aisha did.'

Vertigan smiled. 'I know. You're stronger than we ever were. Now, just do as I do.'

He took a step forward, placing both hands on the rim of the bowl beside the rune of Ulgu. The others followed suit – Scratch felt Alish's fingers brush against his own, the marble cool beneath his palms. But there was a sort of heat there too, a warm tingle that spread up through his arms and

into his body. Shafts of gold broke above the mountain peaks, lighting up the black clouds. A warm note sounded in the air, a rolling peal like birdsong and lapping water and a choral chant rolled into one.

Then the sunlight touched the peak of the fountain and Scratch felt a thrill pass through him, a surge of joy and strength and certainty. He knew in that moment that he was exactly where he needed to be, free and alive, and no longer anyone's pet.

At his side Alish shivered, and as he glanced her way Scratch realised he could sense her thoughts, her feelings blending with his own. Alish looked around the circle, wondering how such mismatched people – a witch hunter, a slave girl, a lord's son, a street fighter, a thief, a lost boy and an inventor – could have formed such an unbreakable bond. Beside her Thanis was feeling stronger than ever before, not just in her muscles but in her mind too. She had protected her friends through all of it, and Scratch could feel her glow with pride.

Elio looked across at Scratch and grinned, gripping the pulsing marble. He was marvelling at how far they'd come, how much they'd achieved. For the first time in his life he felt worthy of his father's name, of the trust Elias had placed in him at the very end. Kaspar felt the power passing from his friends to himself, opening himself up and allowing himself to trust them. It was a completely new feeling.

In Kiri's heart a single word was echoing, a word she'd almost forgotten over the past year, but that had once meant so much to her. The word was *family*, and as she looked around the circle she knew this was it, her family, her tribe, her very own chosen ones. She'd never have to be alone again.

The power grew, coursing through them, and Scratch saw beams of azure radiance arcing from his fingertips, joining with those of Alish and Kaspar, coiling and winding to form a ring of light running right around the fountain's bowl. That single note rang, harmonious and beautiful. Even the noise of battle seemed to have abated.

Then the band of light began to shrink, narrowing around the centre of the fountain, still attached to Scratch and the others by deep blue tendrils of power. It passed through solid stone and there was a rushing sound, a gulping, gurgling rumble that seemed to emanate from somewhere very deep beneath them.

Suddenly the fountain burst open and clear water poured from it, a great cascade gushing up into the sunlight, filling the bowl and spilling over the sides, splashing on the stones of the courtyard. Scratch felt the mist on his face and laughed, giddy with excitement. His hair was soon soaked and his clothes too, but he didn't mind. The torrent increased in strength, arcing so high that droplets stained the red roofs beside the courtyard. Then the wind picked up and he saw the water gusting away, carried out over the city.

Feeling movement around his feet, he looked down. The earth had turned to mud, stirring and bubbling as something emerged from it – green shoots and blades of grass, dark roots and twisting vines, coiling around his bare feet. Behind Vertigan was a tall tree, its branches naked in the sunlight. But as Scratch watched, the grey wood softened to brown, white buds sprouted from dead limbs and new leaves curled open to the sky. All across the courtyard life began to spring up, blooms of every colour imaginable, bursting wide to greet the day. He could smell the sweetness of pollen, and hear the chiming song of birds. It was magical.

Then gradually, another sound reached his ears. This was a darker sound, a deep, unearthly rumbling. The fountain began to tremble, just softly at first

then with increasing force. Vertigan
raised his eyes to the wall of the
palace, his face filled with uncertainty.
The shaking grew more intense, the
floor vibrating beneath them, the
fountain juddering as the water gushed
from its peak.

Scratch released his grip on the marble
bowl, taking a step back. The others
were doing the same, breaking off and
looking around with fear in their eyes.
The buildings enclosing the courtyard
shook, chunks of masonry toppling free
and smashing on the stones beneath.
Then the rumbling turned to tearing,
a jagged, screeching sound like the sky
ripping in two. Scratch turned to see the
entire wall of the building behind him
collapsing inwards, clouds of dust rising.
Beyond it he saw more towers falling, an
entire wing of the Arbour crumbling into
dust. Even the Atheneum began to lean,
the great dome cracking as one wall
subsided, tipping the whole structure off
balance.

And as the walls fell away the city was revealed, the great smoking labyrinth where the golden sky-warriors were still struggling against the Skaven and the skeletons. The outer wall of the Arbour had been breached, corpses swarming over the stone barricade and tearing through the gardens of the palace. The Stormcasts were struggling to hold them back, forming up and striking at the ratmen and the dead.

But they had an ally on their side, Scratch saw. Everywhere he looked patches of green had begun to flourish amid the smoke and darkness, trees blooming in the palace grounds and beyond. Vines snaked from the soil, tripping the unwary skeletons and dragging them down into the earth. Walls of foliage rose to block the Skaven's path, forcing them back towards the waiting Stormcasts. It was as though two mighty forces had been unleashed against one another – the power of life and the power of death, battling not just in the streets of Lifestone and the grounds of the Arbour, but in the very earth itself.

Then a shadow fell and Scratch swallowed. Rising before them he saw the one responsible for all this, the one who had brought death to this living city. Ashnakh floated above the palace grounds, above the buildings she'd torn down, borne aloft by a mass of formless, writhing spectres. Her eyes shone with cold fire, and her laughter rang through the rubble-strewn courtyard.

Vertigan stepped forward, circling the fountain and standing before it with his staff clutched in his hands. His expression was determined but Scratch could see the uncertainty in his eyes. *He doesn't think he can beat her,* the boy realised suddenly. *He knows she's too strong, and he's afraid of what she'll unleash.*

The others lined up on either side of their master, the fountain at their backs. Kiri drew her catapult and Alish clasped her hammer. Thanis braced her steel gloves and Kaspar gripped the music box. Scratch huddled beside Elio, trying to look brave even though his nerves were trembling and his insides had turned to liquid.

'You're too late,' Vertigan told Ashnakh. 'The ritual is over.'

But the sorceress laughed gleefully as she floated closer, cupping her hands and letting the water from the fountain fill them. 'I'm just in time,' she said.

'The Soulspring is open, and waiting for me.' She drank, the water streaming down her chin. But to Scratch's horror he saw that it had turned black, dripping like oil onto her gown.

Vertigan shook his head grimly. 'I won't let you do this,' he said. 'Not again.'

Suddenly he swung the staff, unleashing a wave of power. But it was far too weak and Ashnakh batted it away as though swatting an insect.

'The spring is mine,' she told him. 'I will feed my corruption deep inside, laying the great soul of Lifestone bare for Nagash to claim.'

She raised her face to the spray, the droplets turning black as they touched her skin. Then Scratch saw that the darkness was spreading outwards, flowing back through the falling water, darting from drop to drop like an infection. Soon it would reach the heart of the fountain, passing through the Realmgate and into the Soulspring.

'Deep down, you knew this would happen,' Ashnakh told Vertigan as he raised his staff. 'Death always defeats life in the end.'

'You're wrong,' Vertigan told her, forcing the words out. 'Life endures, no matter what you throw at it. Just like hope, Aisha. And love.' He looked at her through the falling mist, through the spirits coiling around her body and right into her dark, shining eyes. 'I always loved you,' he said. 'Even after everything.'

Scratch watched the sorceress closely, waiting for her face to crack with anger, or disgust, or cruel amusement. But instead Ashnakh simply nodded, clasping her hands together.

'I know,' she said, as a fire-bolt formed in her hands. 'I never stopped loving you either, Mikal. But it doesn't change what I have to do.'

Vertigan gasped, taking an involuntary step back. Scratch could see the shock on his face, the horror and disbelief as her words sank in. He swung the staff up to block the fire-bolt that roared towards him, vast and flaming. But it was much too late.

The fire-bolt struck the witch hunter in the chest, tearing his staff into two jagged pieces and throwing him back against the fountain. He struck it with the force of an explosion, shattering the stones, rupturing the marble bowl, tearing the fountain apart in a wave of violet energy and hideous noise.

CHAPTER NINE

The Music Box

A black rain was falling, drumming
on the earth. Kiri lifted her head, her
ears ringing. Her friends lay scattered
around her, Thanis and Elio and the
others, face down in the mud. She
remembered Vertigan's story and her
heart seized. Had it happened again?

But as she forced herself to her feet
she saw Kaspar's hand twitch, saw him
roll on his belly and try to stand. The
others were doing the same, opening
their eyes, struggling up. Relief washed
over Kiri and she almost sobbed.

But one remained motionless, flat on
his back in the wreck of the fountain,

as dark water rained down around him. She ran to Vertigan's side, taking his hand. But her master did not stir, his eyes lightly closed as the drops beat down on them.

'So sad,' a voice said from behind her. Then Ashnakh sighed. 'I wasn't lying, you know. I truly did love him.'

The sorceress crossed the courtyard towards them, her feet barely touching the stones. She was soaked from head to foot, the spirits still writhing around her body.

Kiri turned, anger boiling inside her. 'You don't love anything,' she spat. 'You don't know what the word means.'

Ashnakh shook her head. 'You can believe that, if it makes it easier. Either way this is over, child. You tried your best, but it's done.'

She glanced back, and beyond the blackened walls Kiri saw that the battle was almost over. Bands of Stormcasts were still fighting hard but they were hopelessly outnumbered, gleaming against the dark mass of Ashnakh's army like tiny golden stars in a pitch-black sky. A knot of nighthaunts descended on one of the warriors, their misted fingers reaching inside her armour and driving her to the ground. Her fellows ran to assist but more spectres rose, falling on the Stormcasts like a pack of ghostly wolves. The sound they made was terrible.

'The Soulspring is mine,' Ashnakh told Kiri. 'Lifestone is mine. I will tear the city apart, street by street and stone by stone. From the rubble I will build a palace, forged from living rock and bound by the souls of all those my army have cut down. The city of Deathstone will be a beacon, a symbol of the power of death over life.'

Kiri wanted to scream at her, to fight back, but deep down she knew there was nothing she could do. Ashnakh was right. She had won.

Then she heard a sound behind her, cutting through the rumble of the battle and the drumming of the rain. It was faint but clear, a high, musical chime increasing in volume as the air grew still. Kiri saw her friends turning in confusion and a figure stepped forward, hooded and cloaked, gripping something in his upraised hands. It was Kaspar, and the box he was holding gleamed with silver light.

'Aisha,' he said. 'Listen.'

The sorceress saw him and frowned, shaking her head. 'Apprentice,' she said. 'What do you have there? What is that hideous sound?'

Kaspar took another step, raising the music box. The chimes grew louder, tiny hammers striking in time with the falling water. 'You remember this, don't you?' he asked. 'Aisha is still in there, somewhere.'

The chimes pierced the air, louder than such a small box should be able to make. And listening, Kiri felt the strangest sensation pass through her.

In her mind she saw her mother's

face, smiling as lantern-light set her dark hair gleaming. She felt the softness of Chetan's hands and heard her voice whispering sweet words, a melody as ancient as Lifestone itself. Kiri knew the song, of course she did. It was part of her, it always had been.

Then a voice sounded, dry and ragged but growing in confidence. Kiri looked around and to her astonishment she saw Scratch with his head thrown back, bellowing out the words in a loud, off-key howl.

'C-c-city of Lifestone, c-c-city of light.
Home of the healers, spirits so bright.'

Kiri heard him and was amazed – Scratch was speaking, no, he was *singing*, and as she listened she heard a second voice joining in. Elio sang awkwardly at first, as though he was only just able to recall the words.

'Though I may wander, though I may roam,
City of Lifestone, call me back home.'

Alish raised her voice and Thanis too,

both of them reaching for Kiri's hands. As she felt the power course through her, Kiri opened her mouth, joining the ragged chorus. Together they turned towards Ashnakh. The sorceress's face twisted with bitterness.

'Be quiet!' she screeched. 'Shut your filthy mouths!'

But now Kaspar was singing too, matching time with the music box.

'City of Lifestone, heart of Ghyran.
Keeper of secrets, shelter of man.'

Looking down Kiri saw light between Kaspar's hands, a shimmering gleam like moonlight on water. It was coming from the music box, from the mirror inside its lid.

'Though long is the battle and dark is the day,
City of Lifestone, show me the way.'

The music box shook in Kaspar's hands as a beam of light shot from it, streaming towards Ashnakh. It surrounded her and she writhed in silent anguish, her eyes pinned wide,

staring into the heart of the mirror.
And through the din of battle, through
the cacophony of their singing, Kiri
heard another sound – childish laughter.
For a moment she was confused, then
it struck her. This was Aisha's voice,
the laughter of the child she had been,
echoing from the deep past and out
into the morning.

Suddenly Kiri realised what the
music box was for, and why it was so
important. It was the only thing Aisha
had kept from her childhood, the only

reminder of the girl she'd been before the old witch-woman adopted her, before Nagash wormed his way into her soul. It contained the last shreds of her innocence.

The sorceress fought against the light that held her, writhing soundlessly. With a gesture she sent two of her wraiths spiralling towards Kaspar, their mouths screaming and their eyes like shards of reflective glass. Kiri and the others leapt to defend him, breaking their grip on one another as the phantoms descended. Alish cried out as one of the spirits took hold of her, clutching at her cloak and pulling her away. She swung her hammer but the phantom simply darted away, cackling.

Kiri could see Ashnakh regaining her power, fighting back against the light from the music box. *It's not enough,* she realised. *We've weakened her, trapped her, now we need to strike the final blow. But how?*

Then Thanis gave a cry, stooping to

lift something from the grass. It was Vertigan's staff, but somehow it was whole again, the two broken shards knotted together with vines and roots, coiled around the mark of Azyr that blazed on its tip.

Thanis ran to the fountain, pressing it into the witch hunter's hand. Kiri saw his eyes fluttering, his mouth working. He looked at the staff in amazement, the vines bursting into flower as he gripped it tight and stumbled to his feet.

'No,' Ashnakh managed, struggling free of the beam of light. 'Don't you—'

With a monumental effort, Vertigan swung the staff. But instead of a blast of energy Kiri saw green shoots exploding from it, a wild emerald tangle that ripped through the air, deadly blooms unfurling. The spirits surrounding Ashnakh shrieked in dismay and fled into the shadows, leaving her exposed. She tried to form a fire-bolt but she was too weak, energy sparking uselessly in her hands. The vines seized her, coiling around her body, gleaming in the light that still streamed from the music box.

Vertigan took a step towards her, the staff clutched in his hands. The vines tugged, drawing Ashnakh closer, hauling her across the ground. She had stopped struggling and her gaze was fixed on his, clear and unblinking. Kiri saw Vertigan smile, his weary face filled with love and forgiveness. The sorceress faced him, tears streaming down her cheeks and mingling with the falling water. It was clear, the poison gone.

Then Ashnakh dropped to her knees and Vertigan staggered too, reaching for her as he fell. They landed side by side in the grass, the water from the Soulspring flowing over them, washing the dirt and the grime and the years from their faces. Aisha's eyes were softly closed, her skin so pale it shone. The stream of water from the fountain began to abate, and in that moment,

Kiri thought, she looked almost peaceful.

Then the ground opened and Aisha began to sink, the vines pulling her in. Kiri watched, and somehow she knew that Lifestone itself was consuming Aisha, drawing her in, reclaiming its wayward child. The earth closed over her and she was gone.

Then the vines came for Vertigan, wrapping around his wrists and his ankles, crimson and blue blooms bursting on his body. He began to sink too, the tendrils pulling him under, and Kiri cried out.

'No!' she shouted, running to her master's side. 'Not him, not yet!'

Thanis joined her and together they clawed at the vines, tugging the pulsating roots away from Vertigan's body. Alish crouched, freeing his ankles, while Scratch and Elio tugged at an arm-thick tendril that had coiled around his waist. Kiri was half expecting the vines to fight back, to resist somehow. But instead they withdrew into the earth, allowing her to drag Vertigan clear, clutching him in her arms.

Kiri laid Vertigan down, tears streaming as she pressed her ear to his chest, listening for his breaths. 'Please,' she muttered. 'It's not his time.'

'Maybe it is,' Kaspar said, standing over her. 'Maybe he's gone.'

'His time is close,' another voice said. 'But it has not come yet.'

Kiri turned, squinting up into the light of the rising sun. A golden figure was approaching through the rubble-strewn courtyard, a huge broadsword swinging at his side. Beyond him Kaspar could see the battle breaking down, the leaderless armies falling back, leaving the grounds of the Arbour strewn with bones and wounded Skaven.

'You have to help him,' Kiri pleaded as the Stormcast strode closer. 'He's a great man, he can't die. He brought us together, and he saved the city.'

'His deeds are known to us,' the warrior said. 'Mikal Vertigan, witch hunter. For many years he guarded Lifestone, alone and unaided. He was a true soldier of Sigmar.'

'Was?' Alish asked, her lip trembling. 'You mean...'

'Not quite,' said a cracked voice, and they looked down. Vertigan's eyes were open, his face drained of colour. He tried to push himself up but he couldn't manage it, slumping back in Kiri's lap.

'Aisha,' he asked. 'Is she...?'

Kiri shook her head. 'She's gone.'

Then the Stormcast's shadow fell over him and Vertigan looked up, their eyes meeting. The old man nodded and the Stormcast nodded back.

Kiri heard Kaspar gasp. 'You're leaving us,' he said. 'Aren't you? You're going to Azyr, to be remade. To become a Stormcast Eternal.'

Vertigan smiled wearily. 'And after

you came all that way to find me.' He coughed, looking up at the children standing over him. 'It is a great honour, to be called by Sigmar. Though I will miss all of you.'

'But you can't leave now,' Thanis said tearily. 'You only just saved Lifestone.'

Vertigan shook his head. 'No,' he said. 'That was you. You stood strong, and you stood together.' He looked from Scratch to Alish, from Kaspar to Thanis, and when his eyes met Elio's the boy gave a choke of grief, weeping openly.

'This war isn't over,' Vertigan told them. 'Not by a long way. There will be many trials to come, many challenges to face. But as long as you're united, I know you'll come through. And we may meet again, though none of us will be the same.'

At last he looked up at Kiri, his eyes creasing with affection and sorrow.

'You have to let me go now, child,' he said. 'Step back, and let me go.'

Kiri started to protest but the Stormcast reached out a gloved hand, beckoning. With a sigh she allowed herself to be drawn to her feet, leaving Vertigan slumped on the ground. For a moment all was silent.

Then a flash of light struck the courtyard, a single bolt of lightning crackling down from the sky. Kiri felt the heat on her face and saw the shape of the bolt burned like a brand on the backs of her lids. When she opened her eyes, Vertigan was gone.

CHAPTER TEN

After All

Kiri hurried up the wide street,
pushing through crowds of excited
people. Houses rose on either side,
their windows thrown wide, the sound
of laughter and song echoing from
within. Above her head the sky was
deepest blue, and from all around
she could hear the clamour of birds
and the rustle of leaves, the sound of
hammers ringing from crackling forges
and shopkeepers crying out their wares.
Lifestone was awake once more.

She thought about everything Master
Vertigan had told them, all those days
ago. The city was a living being, it had

a soul and a spirit and even a mind of its own. She didn't fully understand it, and somehow she suspected she never would. But still, it made a sort of sense to her. The city was alive, and she was part of it.

She reached the prow of the hill and saw the Arbour up ahead, the stone Stormcasts standing in their silent rows. She felt a flush of pride as she remembered those fierce warriors, and how she and her friends had fought alongside them. Beyond them

the white towers rose, those that had escaped Ashnakh's destructive outburst. Figures swarmed over them, stonemasons and builders, even a handful of Duardin, all working to put the old palace back together. She knew Vertigan would've been happy to see it.

The boulevard in front was packed with people, voices filling the air, sharing news and gossip and plans for the future. She thought back to the city she'd first arrived in, sullen and silent and slowly crumbling. That place was gone, faded like a memory.

Then a fanfare blew, piercing and bright, and the crowd fell silent. A troupe of Lifestone Defenders marched through the reforged gates of the Arbour, their fountain breastplates gleaming, their pikes held aloft. Behind them hurried a smaller figure in an oversized suit of armour, blushing as he climbed a wooden podium and faced the people of the city.

'G-greetings,' Elio managed, gripping

the podium to stop his hands from shaking. 'Many of you know me, but for those who don't I am Elio, son of Elias, and by the traditions of this city the new Lord of Lifestone.'

A murmur ran through the crowd and Kiri could sense doubt in the air. They weren't against Elio, not yet. But they weren't completely convinced by him either.

She pushed closer, catching sight of a figure taller than the rest, with flame-red hair under a silver helmet. Thanis was flanked by Kaspar and Scratch, the ragged boy holding tight to Alish's hand. Kiri joined them, waving at Elio and making him blush.

'Our city has been through so much,' he went on. 'We lost our purpose, we even forgot the songs we grew up with. As a result we were left wide open to Ashnakh and her dark army.

'But we came through. With the aid of Sigmar we drove the dead back, and now we find ourselves in a time

of glorious rebirth. All across the city people are remembering who they used to be. Healers and apothecaries and craftsmen are rediscovering the callings they were born to, but had somehow forgotten. Others have returned from distant lands, answering the song of home. The Arbour will be rebuilt, and will once again become a place of learning, of healing, of life.'

There was scattered applause and Elio drew upright, gaining confidence.

'But we cannot forget the darkness

that still holds sway outside our gates. We cannot forget how easily this city can be threatened by those who mean it harm. And we cannot forget those who always watched over us, the ones whose vigilance never wavered.'

Kiri knew he was talking about Vertigan, but also about his father. Both men had given their lives in the defence of Lifestone.

'We must never let such times come again,' Elio said, thrusting out his jaw. 'As long as I am lord, I vow to do all I can to protect our city, to ensure that Lifestone is able to thrive and endure, even in dark times. I call on all of you to help me!'

This time the applause was loud and enthusiastic, echoing from the walls of the Arbour. Kiri found herself clapping along, as Thanis grinned and Scratch whooped and hollered, waving his hands in the air and yelling Elio's name.

'Honestly,' Alish told the boy as the cheers died down. 'I'm not teaching you how to talk just so you can make a spectacle of yourself.'

Scratch grinned at her and she sighed affectionately, wrapping an arm around his shoulders. Together the five of them headed towards the gleaming steel gates, where they found the new lord waiting for them.

'Did I do all right?' Elio asked nervously. 'Do you think they liked me?'

'You were great,' Kaspar said. 'Every inch the young lordling.'

There was the faintest hint of sarcasm in his voice but Elio ignored it, leading them through the flourishing grounds and up towards the palace. A bell began to toll and he quickened his pace, his boots crunching on paths of new-laid gravel.

'I don't want to be late,' he said. 'One of the new healers is giving a lecture on Aqshian fire-herbs, and I don't want to miss it.'

'But you're the lord of everything now,' Thanis said, surprised. 'Why are you still going to lessons?'

'It's not a lesson, it's a symposium,' Elio told her. 'And I'm going because it's interesting. Just because I'm lord doesn't mean I don't still want to be a healer. I'm going to keep learning all I can, and everyone'll just have to get used to it.'

'I'm learning loads too,' Alish said. 'I found a Duardin who said she'd help me repair the *Arbour Seed*, and Scratch is going to be my apprentice, aren't you?'

He grinned excitedly, and Kiri wondered if the boy knew what he'd signed himself up for.

'Well I'm joining the Lifestone Defenders,' Thanis told them proudly. 'The Captain of the Guard wasn't sure, cos I grew up a thief and everything. But after I beat half his first squad at arm wrestling he agreed to give me a trial.'

'I didn't know you all had your lives planned out,' Kiri said, feeling strangely unsettled. 'That just leaves me and Kaspar.'

The boy coughed awkwardly. 'I've actually been thinking,' he said. 'I managed to rescue most of Vertigan's books from the Atheneum. Witch hunter seems like a pretty good profession. I mean, I already defeated one sorceress. With help, of course.'

'Well, that's... that's great,' Kiri said. 'I'm happy for you all.'

'Come on, don't you have any idea what you want to do?' Elio asked. 'You were our leader, you must have some sort of plan.'

Kiri felt her face turn red, and for a moment the urge to run was almost irresistible. She could pack a bag that very night, return to the wild and make her own way just like she'd planned. She'd be alone again, beholden to no one, free of all responsibility...

But then she lifted her head and looked back across the rooftops of Lifestone, the place she'd come to call home. She looked at her friends, all watching her with kindness and concern. And she fought the urge back down, putting any thoughts of leaving out of her mind. She smiled, and shrugged.

'I've got all the time in the world,' she said. 'I'm sure I'll think of something.'

REALMS ARCANA

PART SIX

THE MORTAL REALMS

Each of the Mortal Realms is a world
unto itself, steeped in powerful magic.
Seemingly infinite in size, they contain
limitless possibilities for discovery and
adventure: floating cities and enchanted
woodlands, noble beings and dread
beasts beyond imagination. But in every
corner of every realm, a war rages
between the armies of Order and the
forces of Chaos. This centuries-long
conflict must be won if the realms are
to live in peace and freedom.

AZYR

The Realm of Heavens, where the immortal King Sigmar reigns unchallenged.

AQSHY

The Realm of Fire, a region of mighty volcanoes, molten seas and flaming-hot tempers.

GHYRAN

The Realm of Life, where flourishing forests teem with creatures beyond counting.

CHAMON

The Realm of Metal, where rivers of mercury flow through canyons of steel.

SHYISH

The Realm of Death, a lifeless land where spirits drift through silent, shaded tombs.

GHUR

The Realm of Beasts, where living monstrosities battle for dominance.

HYSH

The Realm of Light, where knowledge and wisdom are prized above all.

ULGU

The Realm of Shadows, a domain of darkness where dread phantoms lurk.

LIFESTONE'S CHOSEN

Lifestone is no ordinary city – much more than just streets, stones and houses, the city is part of a vast living creature, a mysterious being older than time, infusing Lifestone with its soul and its spirit. But every few decades this creature needs to be restored, so once in each generation seven special children are born, each bearing the mark of a different Mortal Realm. When the chosen seven join together a Realmgate is formed, opening a doorway deep into the heart of Ghyran.

THE SOULSPRING

The Soulspring is a well of mystical life-giving water buried far beneath the Realm of Ghyran. The portal to the spring lies in the courtyard of the Arbour, the palace of healing that overlooks the city of Lifestone. The portal is shaped like a stone fountain, carved with the heads of creatures and marked with seven runes. When these runes are activated by the chosen seven, the Realmgate opens and the Soulspring gushes forth, giving new strength to the living city, causing its gardens to bloom and its citizens to rediscover their true purpose.

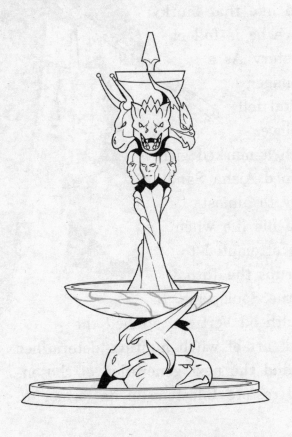

MIKAL VERTIGAN

Mikal Vertigan was
born and raised in
Lifestone, one of the city's
chosen seven. He bears
the mark of Ulgu,
Realm of Shadows,
and like that murky
place he is full of
mystery. As a
teenager,
Mikal fell
in love
with a marked girl
named Aisha Sand,
only to almost
lose his life when
she attempted to
corrupt the Ritual
of the Soulspring. In
adulthood Vertigan studied the
dark art of witch hunting, determined
to find the next generation of chosen,
and restore Lifestone to its former

glory. Nicknamed the Shadowcaster by the common folk of the city, he is a man of many secrets.

WITCH HUNTERS

Grim warriors dedicated to rooting out dark magic wherever they may find it, witch hunters are some of the most mysterious figures in the Mortal Realms. Founded by the noble Wolfgart Krieger, the Order of the Templars of Sigmar is fiercely dedicated to the Immortal King Sigmar, and to the path of righteousness. Witch hunters don't always play by the rules, however, and their methods can sometimes be questionable. Anyone who crosses a witch hunter should expect to pay the price.

AISHA SAND

Like Vertigan, Aisha Sand
was one of Lifestone's chosen,
bearing the mark of Shyish,
the Realm of Death. But
her path was very different
from Mikal's – orphaned
at a young age, Aisha was
adopted by a follower of
Nagash the Necromancer,
and raised to worship the
dark Lord of Death. Trained
in black magic, she planned
to corrupt the Ritual of the
Soulspring, allowing Nagash to
take the soul of Lifestone for
himself. But the powers she
unleashed were too powerful,
and her life was lost. Raised
from the dead by Nagash,
Aisha became the mighty
sorceress Ashnakh, determined
to find the next generation of
chosen and corrupt the ritual
once more.

THE HAMMERS OF SIGMAR

Among the ranks of the Stormcast
Eternals, the mighty soldiers of
Sigmar, one Stormhost is famed and
feared more than any other. The first
Stormcasts to be forged in the fires
of Azyr and the first to
taste battle against the
forces of Chaos, the
Hammers of Sigmar
wear gleaming golden
armour and their
helmets are spiked
like thorned
crowns. Some
wield

swords, others maces — but their chief weapon is the hammer, in honour of Sigmar and his mighty Ghal Maraz. They are said to fear nothing, and their prowess in battle is legendary.

THE DEAD ARMY

Raised by Ashnakh from the corpses of fallen soldiers, the dead army consists of corpse-like deadwalkers, ghastly nighthaunts, undead soulblight vampires and platoons of animated skeletons, all enslaved to the will of their dark mistress. Brought through a Realmgate from Shyish, the Realm of Death, this huge and unruly horde has laid siege to the city of Lifestone, awaiting Ashnakh's order to attack.

THE LIFESTONE DEFENDERS

A noble Freeguild company sworn to protect the city of their birth, the Lifestone Defenders are the last line of defence against the dead army. Led by the Lord of Lifestone, Elias Stonehand, the Defenders will fight to the last man or woman to protect their home. However, the Defenders are not as strong as they once were – as Lifestone has fallen into ruin, their numbers have dwindled and their armouries have been depleted, leaving them vastly outnumbered by Ashnakh's dark forces.

GENERAL BLOODSPEED

The mightiest warrior in Ashnakh's dead army is General Bloodspeed, a soulblight vampire renowned for his supernatural swiftness and his skill with a blade. Even clad in his suit of silver armour, Bloodspeed can move much faster than any other soulblight, making him a formidable opponent. Riding his trained terrorgheist – a winged beast animated by dark magic – Bloodspeed carries the word of Ashnakh to her waiting hordes, giving the order to attack the city of Lifestone.

ABOUT THE AUTHOR

Tom Huddleston is the author of the *Warhammer Adventures: Realm Quest* series, and has also written three instalments in the *Star Wars: Adventures in Wild Space* saga. His other works include the futuristic fantasy adventure story *FloodWorld* and its sequel, *DustRoad*. He lives in East London, and you can find him online at www.tomhuddleston.co.uk.

ABOUT THE ARTISTS

Dan Boultwood is a comic book artist and illustrator from London. When he's not drawing, he collects old shellac records and dances around badly to them in between taking forever to paint his miniatures.

Cole Marchetti is an illustrator and concept artist from California. When he isn't sitting in front of the computer, he enjoys hiking and plein air painting. Warhammer Adventures is his first project working with Games Workshop.

WARPED GALAXIES

An Extract from book one
of the Warped Galaxies series:

Attack of the Necron

by Cavan Scott

Zelia Lor awoke to the sound of
buzzing in her cabin. She groaned.
What time was it? Her bunk creaked
as she turned over, pulling her thick
woollen blanket with her. Surely that
couldn't be the alarm already? The
shrill drone continued, flitting to and
fro near the ceiling. Zelia pulled the
blanket over her head, but the noise
persisted. Throwing back the covers,
she peered up into the gloom.

That was no alarm. There was
something up there, darting back and
forth.

'Hello?' Zelia called out, her voice croaking from lack of sleep. She'd been up late last night, helping her mum catalogue artefacts in the ship's cargo bay.

A series of high-pitched chirps and whistles came from somewhere near the ceiling. Zelia reached out, feeling for the luminator switch next to her bunk. Glow-globes flickered into life, the tiny invader squealing in surprise as it was bathed in sudden light.

Zelia frowned as her eyes focused on her flighty visitor. It was a servo-sprite, one of the small winged robots that her mother used on board their planet-hopper, the *Scriptor*. The whimsical little things had been created by her mother's assistant, Mekki. They had tiny bronze bodies and spindly limbs, with probes and data-connectors for fingers and toes. Their heads were long, with wide optical-beads for eyes that gave the little automata a constant look of surprise. Mesh wings whirred on the robot's back, producing the strident buzz that had woken Zelia.

'What are you doing up there?' Zelia asked, rubbing sleep from her eyes.

The servo-sprite chattered nervously at itself. If Zelia didn't know better she would have thought the thing was agitated, but like all the robots her mother used on their expeditions servo-sprites were just machines. Elise Lor was an explorator, a scholar who travelled the length and breadth of the Imperium excavating technology from years gone by, and who often dreamed of digging up artefacts from the Dark Age of Technology, that period thousands of years ago when machines thought for themselves. Those days were long gone. Like so many things in the 41st millennium, artificial intelligence was a heresy, prohibited by order of the Eternal Emperor himself. While Mekki's creations sometimes acted as if they were alive, they were just following their programming. They were tools, nothing more. However, something must have spooked the little automaton for it to squeeze through the gap beneath her cabin door. Gooseflesh crawled over Zelia's skin. Why would a servo-sprite hide? Something was wrong.

Swinging her legs off the bunk, Zelia gasped as her bare feet touched the cold metal deck. The floors of the *Scriptor* were supposed to be heated, but like most of the systems on the ramshackle spaceship, the heating hadn't worked properly for months. The planet-hopper was old – very old – and its systems often failed faster than Mekki could fix them. But for all its glitches, the *Scriptor* had been Zelia's home since she was born. She knew every creak of the hull, every bleep of the central cogitator. The low thrum of the engines lulled her to sleep every night. They were a comfort, especially during long journeys across the Imperium, rocketing from one dig to another. It was an odd, topsy-turvy life, helping her mum uncover crashed spaceships or ancient machines on distant worlds all across the galaxy, but Zelia wouldn't have it any other way.

But now, the *Scriptor* didn't feel comforting. It felt uneasy, and Zelia had no idea why. Pulling on her jacket and bandolier, Zelia tapped the vox stitched into her sleeve. The communicator beeped, opening a channel to the flight deck.

'Mum? Are you there?'

There was no reply, neither from mum, nor Lexmechanic Erasmus, her mother's archaeological partner and an expert in galactic languages, both ancient and alien. There was no point trying to contact Mekki. Her mum's young assistant was a whizz with technology, but hardly ever spoke to Zelia, even though they were around the same age. At twelve, she was a full year older than Mekki was, but they were largely strangers, the Martian boy preferring the company of his machines. Zelia didn't mind. If she was honest, Mekki made her a little uncomfortable. He was so intense, with his pale skin and cold grey eyes.

Still, he would know what to do with a flustered servo-sprite.

The robot bumbled around her head as she opened the cabin door. She swatted it away, but it stayed close as she stepped out into the corridor. The passageway was quiet, electro-candles spluttering along the creaky walls.

The door to her mum's cabin was ajar, and Zelia could see it was empty. For a woman who spent her life cataloguing artefacts, Elise Lor was incredibly untidy. Curios from her travels were crammed into nooks and crannies, while towers of textbooks and battered data-slates teetered on every available surface. Elise's library was spread throughout the ship, piled high along the narrow gantries. How mum ever found anything was a mystery, and yet she always seemed to be able to put her finger on any text at a moment's notice.

But where was she now? Zelia crept down the corridor, checking Erasmus's cabin, but the elderly scholar was nowhere to be seen. He wasn't in his room or on the mess deck where the *Scriptor*'s crew gathered to eat. Zelia checked the chrono-display on her vox. It was early, barely sunrise. Had mum and Erasmus gone to the dig already?

Zelia jumped at a noise from the back of the ship. Something heavy had been dropped, the deep clang echoing around the planet-hopper. That had to have come from the cargo bay, where Elise stored their most valuable discoveries. They had been on this planet, a remote hive world called Targian, for three months now, and the hold was brimming with ancient tech. Of course, the noise could just have been Mekki, checking through the previous day's finds, but somehow, she knew it wasn't. Mekki was a lot of things, but clumsy wasn't one of them. He would never drop something if he could help it. As the servo-sprite fussed around her head, Zelia picked up a heavy-looking ladle that Elise had used to slop grox stew into their bowls the night before. It wasn't much of a defence, but it would have to do.

Zelia inched towards the cargo bay, praying that she'd find Mekki on the other side of the hold's heavy doors. She paused, listening through the thick metal. There was a flurry of movement on the other side of the door, the scrape of leather against deck-plates, and then silence. Trying to ignore the increasingly frantic buzzing of the servo-sprite, Zelia stepped forwards and the doors wheezed open.

'Hello? Mekki, are you in here?'

There was no answer. The cargo

bay was silent, the lights kept permanently low to protect the more valuable artefacts. She crept through the collection, tall cabinets on either side.

Something moved ahead. Her grip tightened on the ladle.

'Mekki? Seriously, this isn't funny.'

A boot crunched behind her. Zelia whirled around, swinging the ladle.

'You need to be careful,' a gruff voice said. 'You could hurt someone with that!'

Zelia cried out as thick fingers caught her wrist. They squeezed, and the metal spoon clattered to the floor.

'That's better.'

A stranger loomed over her, muscles bunched beneath a scruffy vest festooned with brightly coloured patches. His hair was styled into a lurid green mohawk, a tattoo of a large red cat leaping over his left ear. It was a Runak – a ferocious scavenger native to Targian with

jagged scales instead of fur. Zelia
had only seen the creatures out
on the plains, but imagined they
smelled better than the thug who was
threatening her in her own home.

'Let go of me,' Zelia cried out, trying
to pull away.

'I don't think so, Ladle-Girl,' the
tattooed thug leered, before calling
over his shoulder. 'You can come out.
It's only a little brat.'

Brat? The thug must only have been
a year or two older than Zelia. He
was strong though. There was no way
of breaking his grip. More strangers
slipped out of the shadow – two boys,
and a girl with spiked purple hair
and a glowing eye-implant. They all
wore similar patches on their jackets,
obviously members of the same gang.

'What do you want?' Zelia squeaked,
and her captor smiled, showing
uneven, stained teeth.

'That's a good question.' The thug
glanced around, his small, cruel eyes

scanning the rusting relics on the shelves. 'We thought this place would be full of treasure, didn't we, Talen?'

The ganger behind him nodded. This one wasn't as big, but still looked like he could handle himself in a fight. His blond hair was cropped short at the sides and a small scar ran through one of his thick, dark eyebrows. He held no weapons in his gloved hands, but Zelia couldn't help but notice the snub-nosed beamer hanging next to the leather pouch on his belt.

'That's what you told us, Rizz, but it looks like a load of old junk to me.'

'Yeah, old junk,' Rizz parroted, pulling Zelia closer. 'Where's the real booty? Where've you stashed it?'

'This is all we have,' Zelia told him, glancing down at the hefty weapon Rizz held in his free hand. The ganger had fashioned a mace out of a long girder topped with a blunt slab of corroded metal.

'You like my spud-jacker?' Rizz said,

brandishing the makeshift weapon. 'I call her Splitter. Do you want to know why?'

'I think I can guess,' Zelia replied.

''Cos, I split skulls with her,' he said anyway, as if she were the idiot, not him. 'Ain't that right, Talen?'

The blond-haired juve shifted uncomfortably, glancing nervously at the cargo bay doors. 'We should go, Rizz. There's nothing here.'

Rizz glared at the younger kid. 'Oi. I give the orders. Not you.'

'Then order us to get out of here. We're wasting our time.'

Rizz swung around, nearly pulling Zelia off her feet.

'I'll waste you in a minute,' he growled, brandishing Splitter menacingly.

Zelia saw her chance and took it. She lashed out with her foot, kicking Rizz's shin.